Praise for Daniel Alar
War by Candleli

"Daniel Alarcón's stories are one of the reaso
present worlds we have only imagined or heard about in
poetic ways. And Mr. Alarcón, like the best storytellers, reveals to us that the world we have secreted in our hearts spins in a bigger universe with other hearts just as good and just as bad as our own. Long before you come to the poignant words, 'I come see you, but instead meet your absence,' you will know what I mean."

—Edward P. Jones, author of the Pulitzer Prize–winning *The Known World*

"[T]he most exciting debut in fiction of the year." —Colm Tóibín

"Reader beware: each of the slim tales in *War by Candlelight* starts off innocently enough, but invariably explodes with the fatal power of a grenade or the sudden, magnificent blossoming of a flower. Daniel Alarcón is a storyteller whose wisdom outpaces his youth, and whose talent is already ablaze." —ZZ Packer, author of *Drinking Coffee Elsewhere*

"American literature, whether in English or Spanish, comprises one rowdy, glorious family (as Borges always knew). Daniel Alarcón writes in English, but he reminds me of the young Vargas Llosa. 'Beautiful, disgraced Lima' has a new *enamorado* for this young century, edgy, vibrant, crackling, smart, emotionally devastating, and soaring."

—Francisco Goldman, author of *The Divine Husband*

"[Alarcón's] fierce, stylish, and intricate stories in *War by Candlelight* announce a prodigious talent. . . . His tales, set largely in the hardscrabble world of Lima, build with all power of a Flannery O'Connor story: a gentle enough start, an innocent setting, and before long the reader is adrift in a drama that defies the imagination—with characters that live long after the book is closed." —*Washington Post Book World*

"The sentences are fearless and electric, amplifying the dark joys of the mean streets. . . . His prose is alive with the seen: the large and dramatic but also the peripheral glimpse, like neighborhood kids lacing up their cheap sneakers. . . . Daniel Alarcón is a master delineator of place. When he puts us there, when his city becomes our city, the stunner is that everything is instantly recognizable. That's how we know he has stolen our minds." —*Dallas Morning News*

"However difficult it may be for a person to straddle two cultures, it's an advantage for a writer—an advantage Alarcón exploits with a technical skill and a maturity of feeling that belie his age. . . . Like all good short story writers, he has the gift of compression, of reducing ideas to images. Striking details are what we remember best from *War by Candlelight*."

—*Los Angeles Times*

"[A] raw debut collection filled with dislocated, dutiful souls."

—*Entertainment Weekly*

"*War by Candlelight* is weighty and earnest. There's no doubting Mr. Alarcón's seriousness and ambition. He is one to watch." —*The Economist*

"The engaging stories in Daniel Alarcón's debut collection, *War by Candlelight*, draw on Peru's violent history, the plight of Lima's poor and the hopes of immigrants in New York. They are finely crafted fiction, rich in feelings and images. . . . The stories are vivid with precise details. There's a lot of artistry in these stories, and evidence of a belief in the short story as a perfectly adequate form for illuminating the largeness of life."

—*Chicago Tribune*

"The twenty-eight-year-old Peruvian American writer serves up a richly detailed nine-story debut on the raw tensions and tender mercies common to war and relationships. The author's perceptive takes on his homeland's turbulent past belie his youth." —*Washington Post*

"There is much to admire in Daniel Alarcón's story collection, *War by Candlelight*. Born in Lima, Peru, and raised in the States, Alarcón writes of his native country with a burning youthful ambition that illuminates and inspires." —*San Francisco Chronicle*

"His prose is sinewy, his rhythm's terse, his eye's sharp. . . . At his best, however, in his Peruvian vignettes, he's free of the self-consciousness and trendy, mannered ironies of so many young American writers. Most important, he's got stories you haven't heard before." —*Seattle Weekly*

"Precise, searing language, and immediately embraceable characters. . . . Alarcón's skill with language and his eye for the beautiful tragedy of the human condition are on brilliant display in *War by Candlelight*. Reported to be at work on a novel, Alarcón has given us all a tantalizing appetizer while we wait for our dinner to arrive." —*Minneapolis Star Tribune*

"Alarcón returned to Peru on a Fulbright and now evokes the sorrows and beauty of that ravaged land with a precision and steadiness that stand in inverse proportion to the magnitude of the losses he so powerfully dramatizes. . . . Alarcón, gifted and perceptive, joins a new wave of incisive literary border-crossers."
—*Booklist* (starred review)

"Nine diverse stories show this Peruvian American newcomer's passionate involvement with his material. Whether it's a deadly landslide, a no-holds-barred neighborhood turf war, or a guerrilla war convulsing a nation, Alarcón jumps right in with a fearlessness that becomes his most striking quality. . . . A rare combination of technical accomplishment and generous heart."
—*Kirkus Reviews* (starred review)

"Each of these nine stories provides a dazzling but brief glimpse of Alarcón's talent, which is informed by the natural and political upheavals in his native Peru. . . . Readers will find memorable passages, brutal and lovely, throughout *War by Candlelight*, as the characters do battle with themselves, each other, and the world." —*Boston Phoenix*

"The Peruvian-born Alarcón writes in a strong, vibrant style, with recognizable characters and realistic situations. The names and places are Hispanic in name only; the stories transcend a sense of place." —*Library Journal*

"It was bound to happen: the great new Latin American voice writes in English. Daniel Alarcón's surprising and adrenaline-filled short stories not only put him immediately on the map, they turn the damn map upside down."
—Alberto Fuguet, author of *The Movies of My Life*

"This book is powerful, poetic, and bold. I loved it."
—Chris Offutt, author of *Out of the Woods*

"In Daniel Alarcón's exquisite world, revolutionaries paint brown dogs black because the revolution needs black dogs; a reporter dressed as a clown rides a bus through the streets of Lima; amid buried towns, children chase after aid packages full of neckties. I was so caught up by these lucid stories that I didn't have a chance to anticipate their tremendous elegance. One minute you're riding your bike down the sidewalk in Washington Heights, the next minute, your life has changed forever. Daniel Alarcón is one hell of a writer."

—Lewis Robinson, author of *Officer Friendly and Other Stories*

"*War by Candlelight* is frighteningly unpretentious and direct, as it mines a territory all its own. These stories bare luminous and mundane messages of new worlds with equal aplomb. An inspiring debut."

—Ernesto Quiñonez, author of *Chango's Fire* and *Bodega Dreams*

"In *War by Candlelight,* each story blends with the next so that finally they all seem like plays within one greater play about the natural limits, both personal and historical, of unfair warfare. These stories are knowledgeable and mock sentimentality when they show us how so many occasions in life are merely small rehearsals for death."

—Joe Loya, author of *The Man Who Outgrew His Prison Cell*

"*War by Candlelight* is beautiful and terrifying: a tour through lands, distant and near, where the difference between violence and intimacy blurs. Daniel Alarcón's stories are gritty and compassionate, subtle and unflinching. They carry us straight to the front lines of the struggle for physical and psychic survival, where absurdity and tragedy find equal footing."

—Adam Mansbach, author of *Angry Black White Boy*

"Alarcón's voice is fierce and assured, and his debut collection engages. Every once in a while a young voice emerges with the potential to define a new generation. Daniel Alarcón fits the profile." —*Publishers Weekly*

"The title refers to personal battles—the fight to find one's identity in another country, the fight to be recognized by a lover's family, the fight to live after a soul mate's death. What results are stories that can take on wonderful new meanings in the imagination of any reader." —*New York Post*

"There is a naked honesty in his debut collection, *War by Candlelight*, as characters must decide—sometimes at a very early age—who they are. . . . Alarcón writes with strength and passion. He doesn't try to reconcile two worlds, but instead holds a looking glass up to each." —*Charlotte Observer*

"In Peruvian American writer Daniel Alarcón's debut story collection, *War by Candlelight*, the sights and sounds and tensions of the Peruvian capital come brilliantly alive. . . . There's no denying this is a notable debut by a young author whose sharp, observational eye has some gritty knowledge of human hope and foible behind it." —*Seattle Times*

"A collection marked by buried explosiveness . . . lost love, life-changing decisions, and displacement—Alarcón sometimes has the voice of an old soul. But the author is equally interested in dilemmas faced by his own age group . . . he is tackling subjects well-beyond his years." —*Time Out* (New York)

"Alarcón shows signs that he's on the verge of truly accomplished fiction. Alarcón is an enticing escort into a bewildering world where poverty's strong, democracy's weak, and politics is inescapable. The [collection's] appeal lies in a deft use of metaphor and in underscoring the human aspects of politics, beyond ideology." —*New York Newsday*

"Alarcón writes in a flat, almost affectless way, with an easy touch that makes his hard truths and tragic scenes more palatable: his stories can hurt your heart but his artistry is exhilarating . . . [and] sometimes his spare prose can make you cry." —*San Francisco* magazine

"It is clear that Daniel Alarcón's stories transcend any label. He moves beyond any designation. The stories are by turns gritty and elegant, startling and stunning. Alarcón may have had an extraordinarily auspicious beginning in his publishing career, but it was by no means a fluke. *War by Candlelight* attests to this writer's talents to dangle shadowy visions before us while swooping down to light the way to the next story."

—*San Antonio Express-News*

"[Alarcón] is quickly becoming a writer to watch. . . . The stories are told with unflinching honesty in the face of extraordinary and everyday cruelty."

—*Birmingham News*

"The writing is fluid, the vision unwavering. He soars easily from the slightest detail to an abstract notion and just as smoothly back into the heart of the scene. Most inspiring is the promise that he will continue to shower us with frenzied, wonderful stories in the years to come."

—*Pop Matters*

"Daniel Alarcón may just be one of the best storytellers writing fiction today. His keen eye and amazing descriptions give the stories the kind of detail often lacking in debut fiction. An extraordinary collection." —Bookslut.com

"At an age when most short story writers are in thrall to either Carver-style earnestness or McSweenian irony, Daniel Alarcón is already on another plane. Throughout the book, Alarcón tosses off one casual, beautiful, devastating line after another, announcing the arrival of a Lahiri-like talent to keep an eye on." —*Ruminator Review*

"Stirring. Alarcón's talent is inarguable." —*Philadelphia Star*

"The color and pathos of Alarcón's writing reminds readers of Graham Greene, while his spare language sounds like Hemingway—high praise but deserved. Alarcón talks about war in the street and in the heart, powerful subjects served with finesse." —*Oakland Tribune*

"This confident debut collection of short fiction has much to recommend it: Alarcón is a compassionate new voice whose maturity belies his relative youth."

—*Irish Examiner*

"The stories in *War by Candlelight* are wrenching and powerful. Alarcón's characters never lose their humanity." —*Baton Rouge Advocate*

"Alarcón writes with tremendous humanity and vivid fluidity. His great achievement is to explore the personal consequences of a shrinking world with the same sensitivity and intensity as he considers the established horrors of history." —*International Herald Tribune*

"Alarcón is an urban wordsmith. *War by Candlelight* is a luminous beginning, crackling with attitude." —*The Guardian*

For Paul:
war
by
candlelight
All best!

war by candlelight

STORIES

DANIEL ALARCÓN

NEW YORK • LONDON • TORONTO • SYDNEY

HARPER PERENNIAL

This is a work of fiction. Though the text may refer to specific events or places, they have been freely manipulated or transformed, so that nothing in these pages should be read as history.

Grateful acknowledgment is made to the following publications where these stories first appeared: "Flood," *Tin House* #22; "City of Clowns," *The New Yorker*, June 2003; "A Strong Dead Man," *Glimmer Train*, August 2004; "Lima, Peru, July 28, 1979," *Virginia Quarterly*, Summer 2004; "The Visitor," Los Noveles, Summer 2004.

A hardcover edition of this book was published in 2005 by HarperCollins Publishers.

HarperCollins books may be purchased for educational, business, or sales promotional use. For information please write: Special Markets Department, HarperCollins Publishers, 10 East 53rd Street, New York, NY 10022.

First Harper Perennial edition published in 2006.

Designed by Joy O'Meara

The Library of Congress has catalogued the hardcover edition as follows:

Alarcón, Daniel.
War by candlelight: stories / Daniel Alarcón.—1st ed.
p. cm.
ISBN 0-06-059478-0 (acid-free paper)
1. Lima (Peru)—Fiction. I. Title.

PS3601.L333W37 2005
813'.6—dc22

ISBN-10: 0-06-059480-2 (pbk.)
ISBN-13: 978-0-06-059480-0 (pbk.)

10 ❖/RRD 10 9 8 7 6 5 4 3

For Renato, Graciela, Patricia, and Sylvia:
mi familia y mis mejores amigos

And they've opened your sides to cover their stench
And they've beaten you because you are always stone
And they've thrown you to the abyss so as not to hear
    your voice of fire
And they've wounded you
And they've killed you
And so
    they've abandoned you like an animal
        like the king of any desert
except this one

—CARLOS VILLACORTA, "In Your Kingdom"

contents

war by candlelight

flood

I was fourteen when the lagoon spilled again. It was up in the mountains, at the far edges of our district. Like everything beautiful around here, no one had ever seen it. There was no rain, only thick clouds to announce the coming flood. Then the water came running down the avenue, pavement glistening, taking trash and rock and mud with it through the city and toward the sea. It was the first flood since Lucas had been sent to the University, a year into a five-year bid for assault. The neighborhood went dark and we ran to the avenue to see it: a kind of miracle, a ribbon of gleaming water where the street should have been. A few old cars were lined up, their headlights shining. Street mutts raced around us, barking frantically at the water and the people and the circus of it. Everyone was out, even the gangsters, everyone barefoot and shirtless, moving earth with their hands, forming a dike of mud and rock to keep the water out. Across the avenue those kids from Siglo XX stared at us like they wanted something. They worked on their street and we worked on ours.

"Watch them," Renán said. He was my best friend, Lucas's younger brother. Over in Siglo XX they still had light. I could taste how much I hated them, like blood in my mouth. I would've liked to burn their whole neighborhood down. They had no respect for us without Lucas. They'd beat you with sticks and pipes. They'd shove sand in your mouth and make you sing the national anthem. The week before, Siglo XX had caught Renán waiting for a bus on the wrong side of the street. They'd taken his ball cap and his kicks, left his eye purple and swollen enough to squint through.

Buses grunted up the hill against the tide, honking violently. The men moved wooden boards and armloads of bricks and sandbags, but the water kept coming. Our power came on, a procession of lights dotting the long, sinking slope toward the city. Everyone stopped for a moment and listened to the humming water. The oily skin of the avenue shone orange, and someone raised a cheer.

In the half-light, Renán said he saw one of the kids that got him. He had just the one good eye to see through. "Are you sure?" I asked.

They were just silhouettes. The flood lapped at our ankles, and the work was fierce. Renán was gritting his teeth. He had a rock in his hand. "Hold it," he said.

I felt its weight and passed it to Chochó. We all agreed it was a good rock.

Renán threw it high over the avenue. We watched it disappear, Renán whistling the sinking sound of a bomb falling from the sky. We laughed and didn't see it land.

Then Siglo XX tore across the avenue, a half dozen of them. They were badass kids. They went straight for our dike and wrecked it. It was a suicide mission. Our old men were beating them, then the gangsters too. Arms flailed in the dim lights, Siglo XX struggling to break free. Then their whole neighborhood came and then ours and we fell into the thick fight of it, that inexplicable rush, that drug. We spilled onto the avenue and fought like men, side by side with our fathers and our brothers against their fathers and their brothers. It was a carnival. My hands moved in closed fists and I was in awe of them. I pounded a kid while Chochó held him down. Renán swung his arms like helicopter blades, grinning the whole time, manic. We took some hits and gave some and swore inside we lived for this. If Lucas could have seen us! The water spilled over our broken dike but we didn't care. We couldn't care. We were blind with happiness.

We called it the University because it's where you went when you finished high school. There were two kinds of prisoners there: terrorists and delinquents. The *terrucos* answered to clandestine communiqués and strange ideologies. They gathered in the yard each morning and did military stretches. They sang war songs all day and heckled the young guards. The war was more than ten years old. When news came of a successful attack somewhere in the city, they celebrated.

Lucas was more of a delinquent and so behaved in ways that were easier to comprehend. A kid from Siglo XX caught a bad one and someone said they saw Lucas running across the avenue back to our street. That was enough for five years. He hadn't even killed anyone. They lightened his sentence since he'd been in the army. Before he went in, he made us promise we'd join up when we were old enough. "Best thing I ever did," he said. We spoke idly of things we'd do when he got out, but our street was empty without him. People called us Diablos Jr. because we were just kids. Without Lucas, the gangsters hardly acknowledged us, except to run packages downtown, but that was only occasionally.

Only family was allowed to visit prisoners, but the first time, about a year before the flood, we went with Renán anyway. To keep him company, I suppose, or to gaze at those high walls. We had no older brothers except for Lucas, no one we respected the way we respected him. We thought of Renán as lucky. He could call Lucas blood.

The University was sunk between two dry burnt hills and surrounded by teeming shanties. The people there lived off smuggling weed and coke inside. Everyone knew this, which is why it was one of the safest parts of the city back then. Chochó and I waited outside and smoked cigarettes, looking up at the dull ashen sky. Every half hour or so a guard told us to move out a little farther. He looked uncomfortable with his gun, a little scared. Chochó saluted him, called him Captain.

We talked and smoked and the sky cleared, giving way to bright sun. The third time the guard shooed us away Chochó lit a smoke and offered it to him. Chochó was like that, friendly in his way, though he didn't look it. I knew him well enough to know silence made him nervous. "Come on, friend," Chochó said. "We're good kids."

The guard frowned. He checked the cigarette over suspiciously and then took a deep drag. He looked around to make sure no one had seen him.

Chochó cupped a hand over his eyes. "Our boy is in there visiting his older brother," he said.

The guard nodded. His uniform looked like it could have been his father's: a drab, faded green, too big in the shoulders. *"Terruco?"* he asked.

"No," we said together.

"Those people don't deserve to live."

We nodded in agreement. It's what Lucas had always told us.

"We've got them by the balls," the guard said matter-of-factly.

"Really?" Chochó asked.

"Lucas was in the army," I offered. "Like you."

"And he's in there on some bullshit."

The guard shrugged. "What can you do?"

We were quiet for a moment, then Chochó coughed. "That gun works?" he asked, pointing at the guard's sidearm.

"Yeah," he muttered, blushing. It was clear he'd never used it.

"Tell a joke, Chochó," I said, so the guard wouldn't be embarrassed.

Chochó smiled, closed his eyes for a second. "Okay," he said, "but it's an old one." He looked back and forth between us. "Listen: two soldiers downtown. Almost midnight, a few minutes before curfew and they see a man hurrying home. The first soldier checks his watch. 'He's got five minutes', he says. The second soldier raises his gun and shoots the man dead."

I felt a smile welling up inside me. In the sun, Chochó gleamed like a polished black stone.

"'Why'd you shoot him?' the first soldier says. 'He had five minutes!' 'He lives on my street,' the other one says. 'He won't make it in time.'"

Chochó laughed. Me too. The guard smiled. He stubbed out his smoke and thanked us before going back to his post near the visitors' door. I'm sure he even told us his name, but I don't remember it.

Renán came out awhile later looking beat. He didn't seem like he wanted to talk. We wanted to know everything. The waiting had made us impatient.

"He asked if you were still the same pussies as before, but I lied."

"Thanks."

"No use making him feel bad. I mean, you were born this way."

"Whatever."

"You ask, I tell," Renán muttered.

"What's it like inside?" Chochó asked.

Renán lit a cigarette. "Crowded," he said.

We walked back to the bus in silence. Standing outside did no one any good. It sapped my energy, made me feel helpless. Renán too. "My brother's bored," he said finally. "He's got five more years to go and he's already fucking bored."

"Sorry," I heard myself say.

"He says people start fights just to pass the time."

"Imagine," Chochó said.

Everywhere there was water and the muddy remains of the flood. The clouds broke but the water stayed. A pestilent odor hung in the streets. Summer came on heavy. Some people moved their furniture outside to dry, or set their dank carpets on the roof to catch the sun. They were the unlucky ones. The adrenaline of that night was what would stay, long after everything was dry and clean. My knuckles were still sore and Renán had been hit in the eye again, but it didn't matter.

It was a couple days later when a cruiser pulled up to our street. Two cops got out and asked for the Diablos Jr. There was a mother in the back, a gray-haired woman, staring out the rolled-down window. She pointed at us.

"This punk?" one of the cops asked. He grabbed Renán by the wrist and twisted his arm behind him. I watched my friend crumple. The veins at Renán's temples looked as if they might pop, and tears gathered in the corners of his eyes. "Is this him? Are you sure?" the cop said.

How could she be sure of anything?

"Any other Diablos?" the other cop yelled.

A crowd had gathered, but no one dared to speak.

Renán whimpered.

The cop fired a shot in the air. "Should I name names?" he yelled.

We rode in the back with the woman who had fingered Renán. The windows were up and the heat was a sickening thing. I was sweating against her, but she pulled away from me as if I were diseased. I folded my bruised knuckles into my lap and put on my nice guy voice. "Madam," I asked, "what did we do?"

"Shame," she hissed. She looked straight ahead.

They dropped her off in Siglo XX somewhere. She got out without saying a word. It made me happy to see her furniture was outdoors. One of her sons was seated on the drying couch, his feet up on a rotting wooden table. He snickered when he saw us and blew me a kiss. *Fuck you,* he mouthed silently.

We left Siglo XX and turned onto the avenue, down the hill toward the city. Our neighborhood faded. One of the cops smacked the grille that separated the front seat from the back. "Don't fall asleep back there," he growled. "We're going to the University."

I looked up. Renán snapped to attention. "What did we do?" he cried. It was an old tactic. They were trying to scare us.

"Don't ask me what you did. There's a dead boy in Siglo XX."

"What boy?"

"The dead one."

"You can't take us to the University," Renán said. "We're too young and we didn't do shit."

We screeched to a stop. One of the cops barreled out, and

then our door was open and Renán was gone. I heard him get hit, but I didn't look: it was like the sound of wood cracking. They threw him back in, the side of his face swollen and red.

"Now shut the fuck up," the cop said. We drove.

I remembered the water and the beautiful street battle. The dogs barking and the headlights from passing cars. We'd returned victorious to our flooded streets. No one had died. Even in the harsh disorder of it, I knew no one had died. The cops were lying. We passed neighborhoods that all looked the same: half-built, unpainted houses, every construction a bleached tawny color. The carcasses of buses and cars lined the avenue, the dirt beneath them oily black. Kids played soccer barefoot on the damp side streets, their feet and ankles stained with mud.

When we were younger walking was all we did, along the ridges of the dry mountains, scavenging for things to steal in the streets below. It was safer then, before the war got out of control. Neighborhoods like these stretched on forever, all the way to the city. Once, we climbed the hills above the University and looked over its walls. The delinquents and the terrorists had separate wings. I remember the *terrucos* standing in formation, singing and chanting at the guards that watched them from the towers. Rifles poked out from the turrets. We picked off the prisoners with our fingers, whispering *bang bang,* and imagined them slumping to the ground: shot, bleeding, dead. Lucas had done a tour in the jungle. He'd come with us that day. "The *terrucos* are animals," he said. He blamed them for everything wrong with the country. We all did. It took a while to get used to killing them, he said, and he was scared at first. By the end he was a pro. He carved his name and rank in their backs. "Just because," he said.

He had seven thin scars on his forearm, lines he'd cut himself, one for each kill. He hated the *terrucos,* but he loved the war. He came back home and was respected by everyone: by us, the gangsters, even Siglo XX. He wanted to start a business, he told us, and we would help him. We would own the neighborhood.

We sat in the hills while the *terrucos* sang in the prison courtyard, something incongruously melodic. "I'd kill them all if I could," Lucas said.

"Think of all those stripes," said Renán, holding out his forearm.

Now we turned off the avenue. "I'm thirsty," said Renán. He looked at me as if for support.

"So be thirsty," came a voice from up front.

They put us in a room stinking of urine and smoke. There were names and dates on the walls. In places the stone was falling apart. It was hot. The *terrucos* had scratched slogans into the paint and I could hear them singing. A cop came in. He said that a boy had been hit by a rock. That the rock had broken his skull open and he was dead. "Think about that," the cop said. "He was a kid. Nine years old. How do you feel now?" He spat on the floor as he left. I swear I'd forgotten about the rock until that moment. The flood and then the fight—who could remember how it started?

"I knew it," Renán said.

"No one knows nothing," I told him.

He didn't have it in him to be a killer. If he was thinking about his brother, he didn't say it. I was. I wondered how close Lucas was to us in that moment. In the year since that first visit, I'd written him almost a dozen letters. I wrote about the neighborhood, about girls, and most enthusiastically about joining the army. It's what he might want to hear, I figured, and he would know I hadn't forgotten. It was easy to talk to people who couldn't respond. Renán said they wouldn't give Lucas pen and paper. I knew the truth, though. He'd never learned to write so well.

I put my arm around my friend. "Fuck Siglo XX," I said.

"Yeah," he said, but he sounded defeated.

"Chochó, tell us a joke," I said.

"Ain't nothing funny."

"Fuck you then," said Renán, and we were quiet.

I don't know how long we were there. Every hour or so, a voice would yell that they were bringing new prisoners in, that we should make room. We sat together in one corner, but the iron door never opened. The *terrucos* were chanting in the prison yard. Occasionally, a loudspeaker announcement would make threats, but these were ignored. The air was hot and dank and hard to breathe. We dozed against the dirty wall. Then a man in a suit came in, carrying a stool and a clipboard. He placed the stool in the center of the cell and sat with his hands on his thighs, leaning forward, looking as if he might fall. His black hair was shiny and slick. He introduced himself as Humboldt and asked for our real names. He scanned the papers on his clipboard and coughed loudly into his closed fist. "There are family members outside, you know," he said finally. "Family members of a young man who is dead. They're begging me to let you go so they can kill you themselves. What do you think about that?"

"Let them try," said Chochó.

"They'll tear you limb from limb, I promise you this. You want to go out there?"

"We're not scared," Renán said. "We have families too."

He looked at his notes. "Not so far away, eh?"

"My brother," Renán said, "was in the army."

"That's nice," said Humboldt, smiling. "How did he end up here?"

"He's innocent."

"Incredible. How many kills did he have?"

"Seven," said Renán.

"How many do you have?"

We stared at him, silent.

"Pathetic," Humboldt said. "I'll tell you. You have one between the three of you, that is, until I figure out who threw the rock that killed an innocent nine-year-old. Then I'm going to string you up. You want to know what he looked like? You want to know his name?"

We didn't want to know. Our inquisitor didn't blink.

I had the sickest, emptiest feeling in my stomach. I strained to feel innocent. I imagined a boy sprawled out, down as if struck by lightning, never having seen it or expected it or imagined it: the flood waters of the lagoon running over him, dead, dead, dead.

"You think you're neighborhood war heroes, don't you?"

"We didn't kill anyone," I said.

"What happened to your knuckles?"

I hid them between my legs. "I didn't kill anyone," I said.

Humboldt softened into something like pity. "Do you *know* that? Who threw the rock?"

"There was a fight," Chochó said.

"They came at us," said Renán.

"I know about the fight, and I know you throw rocks like cowards."

"That didn't happen," Renán said.

"You couldn't muster the strength to do it with your hands, like a man would." Humboldt coughed and looked up. "Just like your brother over there. The whore of Pavilion C."

Was he talking about Lucas?

"He's a veteran? What's his name? Your brother? Oh, you didn't know? No wonder the war goes so well, with faggots carrying guns."

Renán tried to lunge at Humboldt, but we held him back. Lucas was a killer. He was brave and made of metal.

Humboldt watched impassively from his stool. "Young man," he said to Renán, "I'll explain something to you. They put common criminals in uniform and call them soldiers, but it never works out. They're only cut out for their little neighborhood scuffles. Men like me win wars."

"Don't listen to him, Renán. He's a suit," Chochó said. "A tool."

Renán glared.

Humboldt smiled coldly at Chochó. "I like you, fat boy. But you don't know dick."

Then he left. "I'm going home to my family," Humboldt said before the iron door shut behind him. "If you ever want to do the same, you should start talking."

We were there a night and another day while our families came up with the bribes. I dreamed we were killers, assassins by chaos, murderers without design. Our city was built for dying. The *terrucos* Lucas fought in the jungle were descending on us. They were in the prison with us, singing their angry songs. We were surrounded. They had their own neighborhoods, places where the cops wouldn't go without the army, and beyond that, places the army wouldn't go at all. Bombs exploded in shopping centers, dynamite attacks assaulted the power grid. *Terrucos* robbed banks and kidnapped judges. Back then it was possible to imagine the war would never end.

Sometime in the middle of the night, Renán woke us up. He was sweating and held a piece of the crumbling wall in his hand.

"Look," he was saying. He ran the sharp edge of it against his forearm, the skin rising in red lines. "I'm going to tell them."

"Go to sleep," Chochó said.

There was no talking to Renán. "They can put me in with Lucas," he whispered. "They can all go to hell."

I wanted to say something, to offer my friend some part of me, but I didn't. My eyes shut on their own. I slept because I had to. The damp floor felt almost warm, and then it was morning.

Humboldt came back in to tell us about ourselves: how we were scum and all the slow and painful ways we deserved to die. He was angry and red-faced. "The human rights people expect me to defend this country with one hand tied behind my back!" he yelled. He said we'd be back when we were older, that he'd be there. Renán hadn't slept. He watched Humboldt, and I knew he was waiting for him to mention Lucas. And I knew if he did, Renán would kill him. Or try to.

But Humboldt seemed to have forgotten Lucas altogether. Somehow, this was even worse. Renán twisted on his haunches. Humboldt rambled on. He spat on the floor and called us names. Then he let us go.

Outside it was sunny, the sky a metallic blue. The earth had baked once again to dust. Our people were waiting for us, our mothers, our fathers, our brothers and sisters. They looked ill.

They thought they'd never see us again. They smothered us with kisses and hugs and we pretended we'd never been afraid. And enough time passed for us to forget we had been. Renán took a few weeks off and then went back to see his brother like he had every Sunday for a year. I wrote Lucas a letter and said I was sorry we hadn't seen him, having been so close. I asked him if he knew Humboldt and which Pavilion he was in. Only four years left, I wrote hopefully, but I scratched that out before I sent it.

I didn't get a letter back.

The rumor around the neighborhood was that there'd been no dead boy that night. People said our rock had struck and killed a dog—a pure breed. It made sense. Two of our neighborhood dogs were poisoned, and then everything was normal again.

Four months passed and the riot started on a Thursday afternoon, on the terrorist side. It was the beginning of the end of the war. Chairs and tables from the cafeteria were set ablaze in the yard. The *terrucos* smoked the guards out of the watchtowers and took some administrators hostage. Weapons had been smuggled in. There was a shootout and black smoke and singing. The *terrucos* were resigned to die. Families gathered outside the University, praying it all ended well. We were there too, learning how to ask God for things we knew we didn't deserve. The *terrucos* burned everything they could and we imagined shooting them. They demanded food and water. The delinquents were starving too, the killers and the thieves and Lucas. They joined the rioting and there were more fires and the guards were killed one by one, their bodies tossed from the towers over the walls of the prison. The authorities surrounded the place. The city gathered on the hills to watch, the smoke twisting black knots in the sky. The *terrucos* hung the flag upside down and wore bandanas over their faces. Whenever anyone moved to retrieve a body, a *terruco* sniped them from the towers. It was on every television, on every radio and newspaper, and we saw it. We sat in the hills. Renán wore his brother's medals pinned to his threadbare T-shirt. His mother and father held pictures of Lucas in uniform. They murmured prayers with hands clasped. Poor son of mine, his mother wailed: Was he hungry? Was he fighting? Was he afraid? We waited. We were there when someone, at the very highest level of government, decided that none of it was worth anything. Not the lives of the hostages, not the lives of the *terrucos* or the rioting thieves, or any of it. The president came on the television to talk about his heavy heart, about the most difficult decision he'd ever had to make. All the hostages were young, he said, and would die for their country. If there were innocents, the president said, it was too late for them now. The moment called for action. There would be no future. And this is how it ended. This is how Lucas died: the helicopters buzzed overhead and the tanks pulled into position. They weren't going to take the University back. They were going to set it on fire. They began the cataclysm. Renán didn't turn away. The walls crumbled to ash and the tanks fired cannon shots. There was singing. The bombs fell and we felt the dry mountains shake.

city of clowns

When I got to the hospital that morning, I found my mother mopping floors. My old man had died the night before and left an outstanding bill for her to deal with. They'd had her working through the night. I settled the debt with an advance the paper had given me. I told her I was sorry and I was. Her face was swollen and red, but she wasn't crying anymore. She introduced me to a tired, sad-looking black woman. "This is Carmela," she said. "Your father's friend. Carmela was mopping with me." My mother looked me in the eye, as if I was supposed to interpret that. I did. I knew exactly who the woman was.

"Oscarcito? I haven't seen you since you were this big," Carmela said, touching the middle of her thigh. She reached for my hand, and I gave it to her reluctantly. Something in that comment bothered me, confused me. When had I ever seen her? I couldn't believe she was standing there in front of me.

At the *velorio,* I picked out my half brothers. I counted three. For twelve years I had insulated myself from my old man's other life—since he left us, right after my fourteenth birthday. Carmela had been his lover, then his common-law wife. Petite, cocoa colored with blue-green eyes, she was prettier than I had imagined.

She wore a simple black dress, nicer than my mother's. We didn't say much, but she smiled at me, glassy-eyed, as she and my mother took turns crying and consoling each other. No one had foreseen the illness that brought my father down.

Carmela's sons were my brothers, that much was clear. There was an air of Don Hugo in all of us: the close-set eyes, the long arms and short legs. They were younger than me, the oldest maybe seventeen, the youngest about eleven. I wondered whether I should approach them, knew, in fact, that as the oldest I should. I didn't. Finally, at the insistence of our mothers, we shook hands. "Oh, the reporter," the oldest one said. He had my old man's smile. I tried to project some kind of authority over them—based on age, I guess, or the fact that they were black, or that I was the *real* son—but I don't think it worked. My heart wasn't in it. They touched my mother with those light, careless touches that speak of a certain intimacy, as if she were a beloved aunt, not the supplanted wife. Even she belonged to them now. Their grief was deeper than mine. Being the first-born of the real marriage meant nothing at all; these people were, in the end, Don Hugo's true family.

At the paper the next day, I didn't mention my father's death to anyone but the obituary guy, whom I asked to run a notice for me, as a favor to my mother. "Is he a relative?" he asked, his voice noncommittal.

"Friend of the family. Help me out, will you?" I handed him a scrap of paper:

Hugo Uribe Banegas, native of Cerro de Pasco, passed into eternal life this past February 2 at the Dos de Mayo

Hospital in Lima. A good friend and husband, he is survived by Doña Marisol Lara de Uribe. May he rest in peace.

I left myself and my brothers out of it. Carmela too. They could run their own obituary, if they wanted, if they could afford it.

In Lima, dying is the local sport. Those who die in phantasmagoric fashion, violently, spectacularly, are celebrated in the fifty-cent papers beneath appropriately gory headlines: DRIVER GETS MELON BURST or NARCO SHOOTOUT, BYSTANDERS EAT LEAD. I don't work at that kind of newspaper, but if I did, I would write those headlines too. Like my father, I never refuse work. I've covered drug busts, double homicides, fires at discos and markets, traffic accidents, bombs in shopping centers. I've profiled corrupt politicians, drunken has-been soccer players, artists who hate the world. But I've never covered the unexpected death of a middle-aged worker in a public hospital. Mourned by his wife. His child. His other wife. Her children.

My father's dying was not news. I knew this, and there was no reason for it to be surprising or troubling. It wasn't, in fact. At the office, I typed my articles and was not bothered by his passing. But that afternoon Villacorta sent me out to do research on clowns, for a Sunday feature on street performers he'd assigned me a few weeks earlier. It may have been the mood I was in, but the idea of it made me sad: clowns with their absurd and artless smiles, their shabby, outlandish clothes. I'd walked only a few blocks when I felt inexplicably assaulted by loss. In the insistent noise of the streets, in the cackling voice of a DJ on the radio, in the glare of the summer sun, it was as if Lima were mocking me, ignoring me, thrusting her indifference at me. A heavyset woman sold red and blond wigs from a wooden cart. A tired clown rested on the curb, cigarette between his lips, and asked me for a light. I didn't have the heart to interview him. The sun seemed to pass straight through me. My tiny family had been dissolved into another grouping, one in which I had no part.

In Lima, my father had settled on construction. He built offices, remodeled houses. He was good with a hammer, could paint and spackle, put up a wall in four hours. He was a plumber and locksmith. A carpenter and welder. When offered a job, he always answered in the same way. "I've done it many times," he'd reassure a contractor while examining a tool he'd never seen before in his life. As a child, I admired my father and his hard work. Progress was something you could measure in our neighborhood: how fast the second floor of your house rose, how quickly you acquired the accoutrements of middle-class life. During the week, he worked on other people's homes; on weekends, he worked on ours. Hard work paid off. We inaugurated a new stereo with a Hector Lavoe tape. We watched the '85 Copa América on a fancy color television.

It was not all that transparent, of course. My father was *vivo,* quick to understand the essential truth of Lima: if there is money to be made, it must be bled from these stone and concrete city blocks. Some win and some lose, and there are ways to tilt the odds. He was charming, and he did good work, but he was always, always looking out for himself.

He was too restless to survive back home. Pasco, where he and my mother and I were born, is neither city nor country. It is isolated and poor, high on a cold Andean *puna*, but in a very specific way, it is urban: its concept of time is mechanized, and no one is spared by capitalism's ticking clock. Pasco is not pastoral or agricultural. Men descend into the earth for ten-hour shifts. Their schedule is monotonous, uniform. They emerge—in the morning, the afternoon, or the evening—and start drinking. The work is brutal and dangerous, and in time, their life above ground begins to resemble life below: the miners take chances, they drink, they cough and expel a tarry black mucous. *The color of money,* they call it, and buy another round of drinks.

My old man wasn't suited to those rituals. Instead he started driving trucks to the coast and into the city. He was twenty-nine when he married my mother, nearly a decade older than his young wife. He'd spent most of his twenties working in Lima, coming back only once every three or four months. Somehow a romance blossomed on his trips home. By the time they married, they'd been a couple for five years already, most of that time apart. I was born six months after the wedding. He went on coming and going for years, making a home for himself in the city, in the district of San Juan de Lurigancho. When my mother would no longer tolerate being left alone, he brought us here too.

That was, I think, the only good thing he did for us. Or for me. When I remember Pasco, that cold high plain, its thin air and sinking houses, I'm grateful to be here. I grew up in Lima. I went to university and landed a respectable job. There is no future in Pasco. Kids don't study and anyway, are taught almost nothing. They inhale glue from brown-paper bags or get drunk in the weak morning light before school. In Lima, the skyline changes, a new building goes up, or one comes crashing down. It's gritty and dangerous, but the city persists. In Pasco, the very mountains move: they're gutted from the inside, stripped of their ore, carted away and reassembled. To see the earth move this way, to know that somehow, everyone you live with is an accomplice to this act; it's too unsettling, too unreal.

I was eight when we moved. My father was a stranger, it seemed, even to my mother. They held hands on the bus to Lima, and I slept in her lap, even though I was too old for that. It was early January; we left Pasco iced over, the syncopated drumming of hail falling on its metal roofs. We watched the speckled orange lights fade behind us, and when I woke up it was dawn and we were pulling into the station in Lima. "There are bad people here," my old man warned us. "Be *mosca,* Chino. You're an *hombrecito* now. You have to take care of your mother."

I'd been to the city before, two years earlier, though I scarcely remembered it. My father had come home to Pasco one day and carried me off for three weeks. He'd led me through the city, pointing at the important buildings; he'd shown me the movement of the streets. I remember my mother telling me that at age six I was already more traveled than she was. Now she held my hand as the world swirled around us, and I watched my old man push his way through the men at the open door of the bus's baggage hold. It was just after dawn. They elbowed and pushed one another, the crowd swelling this way and that, and my father, who was not tall or particularly strong, disappeared into the center of it. My mother and I waited. I stared down a mustachioed man who was circling us, his greedy eyes tugging at the bag my mother had wedged between us. Then there was yelling: one man pushed another, accusing him of trying to steal his packages. The accuser had a foot planted firmly on top of one of his boxes. It was taped, a name and address printed on one side.

"*Oye compadre, que chucha quieres con mis cosas?*"

"*Ah? Perdón, tío,* my mistake."

The second man was my father. It was an accident, he protested. Packages look alike. My father's long arms were bent, palms up, a charmless shrug. But the older man was furious, his face red and his fists clenched. "*No mierda, aquí no hay errores*. Thief!" The other men pulled them apart; in the blur of it, my father grinned at me, and I realized that we'd brought only bags, no boxes.

In front of the Congress, along Avenida Abancay, a protest had spilled off the sidewalk, and traffic was stalled for five city blocks. The protesters were construction workers or telephone workers or obstetricians. Social movements, like all predators, sense weakness: the president was teetering; half his cabinet had resigned. But on the street it still looked like Lima, beautiful, disgraced Lima, unhappy and impervious to change. I'd been to a press conference in the suburbs and was on a bus headed to the city. The air was sticky and as thick as soup. A svelte policewoman in her beige uniform directed cars east, through the miniature streets of Barrios Altos, where cramped *quintas* fell in on each other, where kids laced up their cheap sneakers, scanning the slow-moving traffic for an opportunity. The day before, there had been robberies, entire buses shaken down at a red light, and we were all tense, bags clutched tightly against our chests. It was the first week of carnival, and everyone from age five to fifteen (which, in Barrios Altos, is nearly everyone) was in the streets carrying water balloons, menacing, eager. The dilemma we faced was which way to suffer.

"*Oye, chato.* Close the window."

"*Estas loco.* It's too hot."

The tug-of-war began, between those who were willing to accept the risk of theft or pranks in order to counter the oppressive heat, and those who were not. The driver strained against his homemade seat belt. Windows opened and closed, pulled and pushed from all sides, and on the sidewalks, youths salivated, hands in buckets, kneading water balloons as if they were their best friend's girlfriend's tits. Then it came from everywhere at once: from the narrows between crumbling buildings, and from the roofs as well, kids tossing overhand and underhand, unloading balloons two at a time. Water splashed through the cracked windows. The sidewalks glistened, littered with the exploded insides of red and green and white balloons. The primary target, I soon realized, was not our bus, or any bus, or, as is often the case, a young woman in a white shirt. Instead, on the sidewalk, dodging water balloons, there was a clown.

He was a vender, a traveling salesman, a poor working clown. He'd stepped off a bus and found himself in the crosshairs of a hundred children. He was struggling to get his bearings. He tucked his head into his chest so that his multicolored wig bore the brunt of the attack, strands of pink and red sagging beneath the soaking. He had nowhere to go: a step forward, a step back, a step to the wall, a step to the curb—he danced clumsily in his big clown shoes, the balloons raining on him. There was laughter on our bus, laughter that built community: passengers emerged from their private meditations to point and laugh and ridicule. *Ah Lima!* The clown looked up helplessly, his suit clung to him. The chorus came from the children; to the staccato rhythm of bursting balloons and impatient horns, they sang: *Payaso mojado! Payaso mojado!* Our driver tapped his horn along to it; we crept forward ever so slightly.

Wet clown, the children sang, to the tune of an old Alianza Lima chant. Then the ticket collector, moved by pity, opened the door and pulled the clown in. We fell silent.

He dripped on the corrugated metal floor of our bus, his white face paint running, crinkled pink hairs sticking to his cheeks. It had colored his neck, had stained his clown collar. He made me want to cry, this poor clown, this pathetic specimen of *Limeño. Hermano! Causa!* The bus didn't move, and then it did. The volley of balloons receded. And then, in the uncomfortable silence, disheveled though he was, the clown went to work. He reached into an inside pocket and took out a large plastic bag of mints. Tiny drops of water slipped off the bag. "*Señores y Señoras, Damas y Caballeros,*" he proclaimed. "I'm here today to offer you a new product, a product you may never have seen before. Developed with the newest and most refined technology in European mint processing . . ."

We could still hear the protest on the west side of the Congressional building. Wooden spoons against pots, a dull metallic complaint, rhythmless, the thick voice of the people with their unfocused rage. The disgruntled and disaffected threw stones and burned tires and scattered through the antique streets of the city. The clown in his plastic clown voice tried to sell us mints, his smile a force of will.

The newsroom swarmed with activity; a presidential pronouncement on the economy had set everyone to work. There were rumors: a cabinet member had fled the country. I didn't pay much attention. I left the office early and went to San Juan to see my mother. I took a copy of the paper to show her the obituary, a peace offering of sorts.

San Juan, my old street: the same crooked tree casting thin shadows in the vanishing light of dusk. I'd been living downtown for six years, but I recognized some faces. Don Segundo, from the restaurant, who had fed me for free a hundred times when we were short. Señora Nelida, from the corner, who would never give back our ball if it landed on her roof. Our old neighbor Elisa was there too, sitting, as she always did, on a wooden stool in front of her store. One of the legs was shorter than the others. She'd repaired it with a phone book, wedged between the ground and the offending leg.

"*Vecina,*" I said.

We spoke for a minute, the exchange easy and familiar. What I was doing. My work at the paper. How proud they were of me in the neighborhood when they read my name in print. I knew this last part wasn't true, at least not among the people my age. I'd seen how my old friends looked at me: aware, perhaps, that I had once existed as a part of their world, but dismissive of every claim I could have of belonging there still. We were disappearing fragments of each other's history, fading tracers against a clear night sky.

Finally Elisa said, "Your mother's not home, Chino."

The streetlights had come on, and I noticed with some surprise that they crawled up the mountainside now. The neighborhood was still growing. New people arrived every day, as we once had, with bags and boxes and hopes, to construct a life in the city. We'd been lucky. Our new house had been small but well built. Everyone had welcomed us. Our street was overflowing with children, and within a week I'd forgotten about Pasco, about the friends I'd left there. My mother found work as a maid in San Borja, four days a week at the Azcárates', a friendly couple with a son my age. Her employers were generous, kind, and understanding to a fault, especially after Don Hugo left us. They lent us money and helped pay for me to study when my old man abandoned that responsibility as well. They never kept her late—so where was she?

Elisa looked at me somewhat sheepishly. "You know, Chino, she's been staying with *la negra*. With Carmela's family, in La Victoria."

"How long?"

"Since your father got sick, Chino."

Elisa motioned for me not to leave while she sold a kilo of sugar to an elderly woman in a light-green dress. I'd rolled the newspaper into a tight baton. Now I tapped it against my thigh. I considered Elisa's news, what it meant. The scope of my mother's weakness, her astounding lack of pride. How could the arrangement work on either side, especially now, with the man who connected these two women dead? Carmela ran a dress shop, an enterprise she'd begun with my father's investment. With *my* money probably, which should have been spent on *my* books, on *my* schooling. The business had succeeded, but was it enough, I wondered, to support the grief of two widows and three children—two of whom, at least, were still in school?

Elisa turned to me again as her customer shuffled down the street.

"Does she come here then? Ever?" I asked.

"Your mother? Sometimes. I saw her a few days ago. I don't ask so much, you know. She's embarrassed. She's afraid of what you'll think."

"She knows exactly what I think."

Elisa sighed. "She didn't want you to know."

"Then you shouldn't have told me."

Elisa leaned back against the metal gate in front of her store. "Oscar."

"I'm sorry, *vecina*." I looked down at my feet like a misbehaving child, and stamped out the prints of my sneakers in the dusty earth. "Anyway, thank you."

"I'll tell her you came by when I see her. Or you know, Chino, if you want you could—"

"Thank you, *vecina*."

It was late. From my old street, I used to cut across the field behind the market, at any hour, fearlessly, but now it was an unnecessary hazard. The addicts would be out. In the firelight flicker of their ritual, I might have recognized an old friend, ashen, lost. I walked the long way out to the avenue.

I tried to picture my mother in her new home, sleeping on the guest bed or on a cot that she put away each morning. She and Carmela, sharing stories and tears, forgiving the old man in a nostalgic widows' duet. What could they have in common? Carmela was *Limeña*, a businesswoman; she knew how the city worked. My mother had been just a girl when she met my old man, barely fifteen. In Lima, he had learned to dance salsa. To drink and smoke, to fight, fuck, and steal. My mother had learned none of this. She had waited for Hugo to come home and propose. Even now, she still had her mountain accent. For years she had known only one bus line—"the big green bus," she called it—that took her to the Azcárates' home. What could Carmela and my mother share besides a battleground? My mother had capitulated. It gave me vertigo. It was the kind of humiliation only a life like hers could prepare you for.

On Saturdays, when we first moved to the city, she would

take me to the Azcárates house with her. We rode that big green bus, my mother tense, watching the streets pass in gray monotony, afraid of missing her stop. As a child and not an employee, I was able to cross certain lines. The Azcárates' were permissive with me, and I never felt out of place in their home. I'd lay out my books on the table in the garden and do my homework, humming songs to myself. Sometimes their son, Sebastián, and I would wage war, setting up epic battles with swarms of plastic soldiers.

My mother liked everything about being in that house. She liked the order of it. She liked the plush of the golden brown carpet. She even liked the books, though she couldn't read them, for the progress they represented. If I was bothering her in the kitchen, she always shooed me away: "Go grab a book, Chino. I'm busy right now."

I was sitting with her in the kitchen one day when I asked her why we had moved. In the comfort of that kitchen, I knew that *this* was better than *that*, but the way my mother spoke of Pasco sometimes, one might picture a wide, fertile valley with temperate climate and warm people, instead of the poor and violent mining town it really was. Lima frightened her. She felt safe in exactly two places: our house and the Azcárates' house.

"We had to move, Chino. Your father was here." She was baking a cake and stirred the mix with a spatula. "Do you miss Pasco?"

I didn't have to think about it. "No," I said. "Do you miss it, Ma?"

"Of course," she said.

"Why?"

Her face fell. "Your grandparents are there! I grew up there! Chino, how can you ask such a thing?"

"I don't know," I said, because I didn't. She was a mystery to me, romanticizing the life we'd left behind. "It's cold there."

"If you lived away from me, wouldn't you miss me?" she asked.

"Of course, Ma."

"That's how I feel."

"Why don't they come to Lima?" I asked.

"Ay, Chino, they're too old. They wouldn't like it here. Lima is too big. I'll never get used to it."

"Papi doesn't miss Pasco."

She smiled. Lima was his backyard, the place where he could become what he'd always imagined himself to be. "He's different," she said finally. "And you, Chino," she added, "you're just like your father."

I sat on the Jirón, watching Lima pass by. A pedestrian mall of roast chicken joints and tattoo parlors, of stolen watches and burned CDs. Colonial buildings plastered over with billboards and advertisements. Jeans made at Gamarra to look like Levi's; sneakers made in Llaoca to look like Adidas. A din of conversations and transactions: dollars for sale; slot machines; English tapes announcing, "*Mano*"—pause, pause—"*Hand.*" Blind musicians singing songs. Pickpockets scoping tourists. The city inhaling.

I'd read my father's short obituary over and over, read it against the other news of the day, looking for connections, for overlaps, for sense. The privilege of being a journalist, of knowing how close to the precipice we really were, hardly seemed worth it at times. The president seemed dazed and disoriented before the press. Ministers disappeared on midnight charters to

Florida. Life moved. I watched a cop take a bribe in the privacy of a recessed doorway. A nun tried to pin a ribbon on me, for a donation. I dodged her with my most polite smile.

Then, from the Plaza San Martín, the whole world was running toward me, and past me on to the Plaza Mayor. Metal gates closed with clangs and crashes all along the Jirón. Business were shuttered with customers inside. The cop disappeared. I imagined the worst: a drunken mob of soccer fans wrecking and looting, raping and robbing. I ran to the end of the block and watched the people scatter. Then the Jirón was empty, and before me was one of the strangest things I'd ever seen.

Fifteen shoeshine boys.

The children walked in rows of three, dressed in secondhand clothes, sneakers worn at the heels, donated t-shirts with American logos. Some were so young they were dwarfed by their kits. One dragged his wooden box behind him, unconcerned as it bumped and bounced along the cobblestones. All were skinny, fragile, and smiling. As they marched toward me, they were led by a clown on stilts, twice their height, dancing elegantly around them in looping figure eights, arms extended like the flapping wings of a bird.

I was seeing a girl once, Carla, who'd worn stilts in a church youth group circus, who needed them in fact, whose little hands and feet and breasts and legs soon lost their charm for me. Nude, she was so compact as to appear almost stout. Dressed, she manipulated her form in tight jeans and tighter spandex tops. Her body flopped and sagged as she undressed, and she would stand slump-backed before me, a little ashamed. Carla lived in San Miguel, near the water. We would go to the ocean sometimes and look at the flumes of gray brackish water pushing out into the sea in curlicues, Lima's broken covenant with water. Once she brought along her stilts, which she claimed not to have used in years. She was beginning to bore me at that point, but I'd never seen someone on stilts up close, or dated a woman taller than me. I helped her up on them, and suddenly she was imposing, half a body above me. Gone was the timid and cautious girl I knew. Everything about her seemed larger, fuller. Her face was lost in the glaze of the setting sun. She was a monument. She waltzed along the gravel, patting me on the head, and I was a child again. From below, her breasts seemed bigger, her hips more slender. She laughed carelessly. I reached up and grabbed her thighs, dug my fingers into her stately flesh. She was on the verge of toppling over but I held her. I pulled her zipper down with my teeth, buried my face in her crotch, and worshipped this majestic woman before me.

Now I watched in amazement as the protest strode past me, the children whispering their demands, the panic subsiding. Had it been a drill? A joke of some sort? Store owners and customers emerged from their bunkers, relieved and confused. Lima was playing tricks again.

I was twelve when I learned my old man had another angle. The scheme went like this: you put in a new bathroom, or tile a kitchen, or add a third floor to a house in Surco or La Molina. You are a model worker, always polite and respectful. You don't play your music too loud. You wipe your feet and clean up after yourself. All the while, you do your real work with your eyes: Television, *check*. Stereo, *check*. Computer, *check*. Jewelry, *check*. Anything electric can be sold: kitchen appliances, even wall clocks. Nice clothes too, especially women's. You scout for windows without locks, flimsy doors, back entrances. You keep track of schedules: when the husband is at work, when the wife is at the salon. When the kids come home from school. When the maid is there alone.

My father and his crew were smart. They could wait a few months or as long as a year. Sometimes the neighborhood security guard was in on it too; for a small fee, he could tell you when a family was out of town. Other times, the maid got the worst of it: the fright, and often the blame.

I remember one evening at our house. They were planning, or, perhaps, celebrating. There were six of them, and I knew some so well I called them *tío*. They came around a lot, to drink with my old man, to play soccer on Sundays. And they sat close together, talking in low voices, bubbling now and then into laughter. I was called to bring more beer from the fridge. I passed the cold bottle to my father, who took it without looking, intent on what his partner Felipe was saying. I listened too: "I always try to smack the maid real good," Felipe said proudly. "And I try to break something—just so the family doesn't think she was in on it." Everyone cheered this perverse generosity. My father too. I stood at the edge of the circle of men as they passed the beer around. I hardly understood it. Standing at the edge of the circle of men, I thought of my own mother falling to the floor.

On Valentine's Day I treated myself to a hooker. In honor of my old man, I suppose. It fell on a Sunday, so lovers had the whole day to make out in the parks, hands furtively sneaking beneath blouses, thumb and forefinger greedily undoing buttons. Lima is an industrious city, even on holiday. The whores work overtime because they know how we are. I didn't feel especially lonely—my life is what it is—but I found myself walking that evening, distracted, unsure of what I was looking for exactly. I told myself I was going out for some air. And I was, ambling through the city, down Avenida Tacna, past the slot machines and the vagrants asleep on benches. It was still crowded out: the sidewalks full, eddies of transients milling at the corners. The cars to Callao honked their horns, calling for passengers. And there the parade began: tall, short, fat, skinny, old, young. Beneath every arched doorway, or leaning against the dirty walls: *chinas, cholas, morenas y negras.*

They don't say anything; they watch you watching them. And you do. And I did. It occurred to me that I wanted to get laid. The idea made me smile. I paid them more attention, and walked slowly and waited for one to catch my eye.

I used to think my old man met Carmela this way. That he picked her out from a runway of prostitutes, whores on parade, eager for an affair with a confident and smiling, hardworking thief. That logic suited my anger: his new wife, a common prostitute. It didn't happen that way of course. Maybe he loved Carmela. Maybe she made him feel things my mother didn't. I don't care. You don't do that shit. You sleep around. You fuck another woman in the anonymous dark of a rented hotel room. You drink with your friends and tell them all about it and laugh and laugh and laugh. But do you fall in love? Do you let yourself be drawn into a parallel life, another marriage, another commitment?

You go home to your wife. You live with the decisions you made.

"What you looking at, *muchachón*?"

My reverie ended. The whore licked her lips.

"Your ass, *niña,*" I said, and she smiled slyly.

"You can do more than look, you know."

It was my turn to smile. I checked my pocket for money, felt the tattered edges of a single worn bill. It would be enough. The avenue was dark, only half-lit by the orange street lamps. I squinted and stepped toward her. She was a beautiful *negrita*. She wore a tight blue tank top, generously revealing. One of the straps hung off her shoulder just slightly. The whore put her hand on my stomach, her palm flat against my shirt. The sharp edges of her nails ran up and down against my skin. They were painted red. Her smile was about the dirtiest thing I'd ever seen. The city had emptied and there was only us.

"Let's go," I said.

Villacorta was asking for his article. I was avoiding him. The government had not fallen, and the protests continued. A group of unemployed textile workers burned tires and looted in El Agustino. There was talk of the president not returning from his next state trip. I was counting on the story to snowball, to crowd my clown feature out of the news section the following Sunday. An extra week would help.

I worked and slept and worked, and thought as little as possible about my old man, my mother, Carmela. I thought about clowns. They had become, to my surprise, a kind of refuge. Once I started looking for them, I found them everywhere. They organized the city for me: buses, street corners, plazas. They suited my mood. Appropriating the absurd, embracing shame, they transformed it. *Laugh at me. Humiliate me. And when you do, I've won.* Lima was, in fact and in spirit, a city of clowns.

The February heat smothered the city, even after dark, and in the evenings, I rarely made it farther than the bar downstairs. The overhead fans whirled, stirring the warmth. I liked listening to the hum of a dozen separate conversations, to the clink of glasses, to cheerful applause in the back room. It made me feel less alone.

One night, a clown stood at the counter next to me. I recognized him. He worked mornings in front of San Francisco, for the children who went there on school trips. I knew the red-and-orange plaid of his suit. Usually he had a partner, but he was alone now, tired, halfway out of costume, headed for home. Like me, he probably wanted a drink to help him sleep. I should have let him go on his way, but before I realized it, I'd blurted out, "You're a clown."

He turned, puzzled, and looked me in the eye. "You asking me or telling me, *causa*?"

"Asking, friend."

"And who the fuck are you?" His frown was very un-clown-like, the kind of look that would frighten a child. There was white greasepaint ground into the wrinkles at the edges of his mouth.

"Oscar Uribe," I said. "I write for *El Clarín.*"

"The newspaper?" He turned away now, back to the business of ordering a drink. I pulled out two chairs at a table by the bar and moved my bottle of red wine.

"Maestro!" I called to the waiter. "Another glass, please!" The waiter acknowledged me with a wave. I looked back at the clown, motioning to the empty chair. He shrugged and sat.

His name was Tonio, he said, and he didn't have all night.

But I kept the wine coming. I found myself telling him about my mother, about my old man. About Pasco and San Juan. He listened and drank. Then he told me about his hometown in the north, about arriving in Lima penniless. He said he'd lived under the Santa Rosa Bridge. And clowning? "It's work, brother. Better than some, worse than others," he said. "I'm not good at much else. It's either this or stealing."

"Amen," I said.

He told me how good it felt to be someone else for a living, to be out in the streets on a clear day. He said the children had sweet faces and it touched him to see them happy. He complained about having to compete with every out-of-work nobody selling candy on buses.

"Does it pay the bills?"

"I don't need much," he said, nodding. "No wife. No kids."

"How did you settle on this work?"

He smiled then so unexpectedly I thought he had misunderstood me. And it was a wonderful smile, a real clown smile. With his thumb, he rubbed at the paint still hiding in the creases of his face. His expression told me I had it all wrong. "No *causa*," he said, shaking his head. "It's like this: you wake up one morning, and *boom!* you're a clown."

Señor Ingeniero Hubert Azcárate opened the door. He shook my father's hand, patted me on the head, and waved us both in. I wiped my feet three times, back and forth against the heavy doormat. I'd been there many more times than my father had. He was watching my every move. There were three stairs, and at the bottom of the landing the room opened up into a wide, airy space full of light. An L-shaped sofa and a leather armchair were positioned around a wooden coffee table. Built-in shelves along the walls held hundreds of books. I'd looked through them before. Read many. The windows looked out on a garden terrace with trees and grass and flowers sprouting in warm colors.

"Mari!" Señor Azcárate called out. "Your husband is here, with Chino!"

My mother appeared from the kitchen, a little shocked to see us. Her maid's uniform was a pristine white. She kissed us both on the cheek, and then she asked, concerned, "What are you doing here?"

Señor Azcárate had already found his way to his comfortable leather chair, and he sat now, observing us with an air of patrician benevolence. "Oh don't worry, Mari," he said. "Your husband only wanted to speak to me. It's no problem at all."

"Go on back to the kitchen," my father said. "We'll come say good-bye before we leave."

"But, Mari," Señor Azcárate called. "Bring me some coffee. You know how I take it. Would you like coffee, Hugo?"

"Oh no, thank you."

"It's no trouble. Really. Mari, bring two coffees." She nodded and left.

My father sat down. He began by recounting reasons we were grateful to Señor and the Azcárate family. The generosity, the solidarity, the understanding. "Things haven't always been easy, but I always tell Mari, I tell her every day, God was smiling on us the day she got this job."

I had never heard my father invoke God for any reason other than to explain the weather.

Señor Azcárate nodded, *yes yes yes*, savoring my father's gratitude. He was a thin man, whose pale blue eyes had become even more prominent as his hair had receded. He often squinted when he spoke, as if we were drifting away and he might lose sight of us. "Please, please, Hugo. Go on."

"Señor Ingeniero, at Chino's new school," my father continued, "everyone will have money." I was about to start at a private school in San Isidro, where the Azcárates had arranged a scholarship.

"Are you worried about the tuition?" Señor Azcárate asked. "I explained to Mari that everything is covered except the uniforms."

"No, no, it's not that." My old man searched for the right words. "You know, Señor Ingeniero, I'm a builder. I work almost every day—I should say, every day that I can." He put his arm around me. "We're so proud of Chino. I always knew that he was a smart one. But, you know, we struggle to pay for this, to pay for that. There isn't always work, that's the thing. . . . I'm embarrassed to even ask, after all you've done for us."

"No, no, ask, Hugo, please." Señor Azcárate leaned toward my father. My father's silence was studied. "How long has Marisol worked with us?" Azcárate asked. "I'll tell you: long enough so that she's family." He smiled, then turned to me, speaking as if to a child of five. "You're family, Chino, you know that? Your father, he's family too."

I nodded, perplexed. Finally, my old man spoke, and this time he went straight to the point. "I was hoping, if it's possible, if anyone from Chino's new school would be doing work on their house . . ."

"I really couldn't say."

"No, but if they were, could you put in a word for me? For my business?"

It was Don Hubert Azcárate's favorite kind of favor: the kind he could fulfill. The kind that confirmed his own charity. He was a nice man, he really was. He promised that he would. My father smiled happily. "Thank Señor Azcárate, Chino," he told me. I shook the engineer's veiny hand. Then my father thanked him effusively. The two men embraced. "You don't know what this means to me," my old man said.

My mother appeared with the coffee.

All my life, I've been Chino. In Pasco, in Lima. At home, in my neighborhood. The way some people are Chato or Cholo or Negro. I hear those two syllables and look up. There are thousands of us, of course, perhaps hundreds of thousands, here and everywhere that Spanish is spoken. No nickname could be less original. There are soccer players and singers known as Chino. One of our crooked presidents lived and died by his moniker: *chino de mierda.* Still, it is my name, and always was my name. Until I started at Peruano Británico. There, I was called Piraña.

Piranhas were already a phenomenon in Lima by the time I started high school. The authorities had ordered investigations and organized police sweeps. There were news reports and shocking images. A city on the brink. In packs of fifteen or twenty, they would swarm a car and swiftly, ruthlessly undress it. Hubcaps, mirrors, lights. The crawling commute held the prey in place—the owner of the car, helpless, honking his horn frantically, aware perhaps that the wisest thing was to do nothing at all. To wait for them to pass. But that was only an option for a while. More audacious crews started breaking windows, taking briefcases, cell phones, watches, sunglasses, radios. *Full service,* people joked darkly. A new kind of crime, sociologists said. And an astute observer—of the kind who traffic in phrases—named them piranhas.

At morning roll call in the courtyard of my new school, my

class lined up single file. I found my place in the order of last names, Uribe, almost at the back. Ugaz in front of me. Ventosilla behind me. My uniform was neat and pressed and I looked, from a distance perhaps, just like all the others. The teacher called us off, and one by one we marched to our new classroom. It wasn't until recess that afternoon that my classmates sought me out. "*Oye*, you play?" The kid held a soccer ball in his hands. He kicked it to me. I passed it back, making sure I used good form. I introduced myself as Oscar or Chino. "César," he answered. We formed a team. We grabbed a kid with glasses and put him in goal. We played. We scored and were scored on. We yelled and sweated and cursed and then, when I took the ball from a kid on the other team, he called a foul, dropping to the floor, and held his ankle, grimacing. In San Juan, I would have called him a pussy, and that would've been that. But he yelled, *"Oye! Oye!"* and we stopped. "That's a foul here, *huevón,*" he said, frowning. "Where the hell are you from?"

I didn't have to respond, but I did. I could have said any place in the city, but I didn't. "San Juan de Lurigancho," I answered.

Of course, eventually they would have found out where I was from. They would have seen me walking back to the Avenida Arequipa to catch the bus home. They would have known that I didn't live in La Molina or Surco. But perhaps if they hadn't learned this detail on the very first day, if they had known me better, they wouldn't have associated me with the criminal reputation of my district.

"San Juan?" he said, breaking into a cruel smile. *"Oooooohh . . . Habla Piraña!"*

I met Tonio the next morning at eight-thirty in front of San Francisco. He was already painted and dressed. I was still shaking off sleep and a red wine headache. He introduced me to his partner, a yellow-faced clown named Jhon.

"You're the reporter?" Jhon asked suspiciously.

"Be nice," said Tonio.

He pulled an oversize polka-dotted suit from his backpack. It was white with green dots. It fit me like a garbage bag. Tonio declared it perfect. Jhon agreed. A pair of green shoes was next; I wiggled my feet into them. They were twice the length of my forearm. Then Tonio handed me a mirror and three plastic canisters of face paint, each the size of a roll of film. "You take care of that," he said, holding out a thin brush.

I felt outside of myself, the details of the previous night's conversation so hazy and wine soaked, I couldn't recall exactly how I had ended up there or what commitments I had made. In the mirror, I watched myself transform. I put red circles on my cheeks. Jhon passed me a nose. It was an oversize red Ping-Pong ball cut in half and threaded by a rubber band. It fit nicely. Finally, Tonio pulled a worn jester's hat from the bottom of his bag. The pointy edges fell limply in my face. It would have to do.

Walking through the city, one-third of a trio of clowns, I was surprised to find how relaxed I was, and how invisible. You'd think the world's gazes would congregate upon us, on our loud costumes and our hand-painted smiles, but most people simply ignored us, walked past without a glance; only children smiled and pointed, sometimes waved. Jhon and Tonio chatted about soccer, I watched and listened in a daydream. We were ghosts in the multitude, three more citizen-employees of the great city, awake and alive on a Thursday morning.

We let a few buses pass because they were too empty. "It's

bad luck at the beginning of the day," Tonio explained. Finally, Tonio nodded as a more crowded bus approached. We pushed past the ticket collector and were instantly onstage, all eyes on us. *"Señores y Señoras, Damas y Caballeros!"* We stood in a row, Tonio in the center, yelling over the asthmatic rattle of the engine. "I am not here asking for charity! In fact, I am a rich man! This is my bus! This is my driver! And *this,*" Tonio bellowed, pointing to the ticket collector, hanging halfway out the bus door, calling the route, "*this* is my mascot!"

Jhon was the chorus, echoing every pronouncement Tonio made, in the stereotypical voice of a drunk lifted from a Rubén Blades song. He pretended to fall, and Tonio made sheepish apologies for his drunken partner, who had spent the night before "celebrating the purchase of a new three-story home in San Borja!"

I felt useless. I flashed my dumb clown smile and tapped my fingers against my chest. I could feel my face paint drying to an uncomfortable film, affixing an unnatural contortion to the muscles of my face. I was dazed, almost seasick, as the bus sped along the avenue. They were talking but I could barely hear them. Tonio was wrapping up. "My humble servant—God bless the poor deaf-mute—will be passing by your seats now to collect your fare." He bowed low and then nodded at me.

We weren't selling anything; this was a bold conceit Tonio had devised to cut costs. It was *our* bus; I passed down the aisle, collecting everyone's fare. *"Pasajes, pasajes a la mano,"* I murmured, just as a ticket collector would. Some passengers, napping, barely opening their eyes, handed me a coin without thinking. Some dropped loose change in my hand, some even thanked me. Most ignored me, looking away, even men and women who had watched the act and smiled.

I collected a total of 4.20 soles. The bus stopped. "Ladies and Gentlemen, good day!" Tonio shouted. We stepped into the morning sun. The whole thing had taken five minutes.

I put a coin in the slot and dialed the number to Elisa's bodega. It was early afternoon. Tonio and Jhon sat in a café across the street, sharing a cup of tea. We were back downtown, taking a break. We'd been thrown off buses, had change tossed at us, been spat at. But we'd made money. A good day, Tonio assured me, better than usual. They seemed content.

The phone rang and rang in San Juan, and then she answered. She asked me how I was.

I looked at the busy street, the people meandering homeward or workward. "I'm at the office, *vecina,* I can't talk long." I asked her if she'd seen my mother.

"At the funeral, Chino. Why weren't you there?"

"I had to work. I couldn't make it. Did she say anything?"

"She misses you, Chino." I heard Elisa sigh. "She said that everything is good with Carmela. That she might sell the house."

I didn't say anything.

"Chino, are you there?"

"I'm here."

"Are you going to visit her?"

Tonio and Jhon were paying with change, haggling for a little extra hot water. They counted the money out in ten-cent coins. The waitress tried to hold back a smile. Jhon leaned over the counter and blew her a kiss. They were charming clowns. "Thank you, *vecina,*" I said and hung up the phone.

My new nickname both labeled me as dangerous and emasculated me. I was never scary to them. I was a joke. I represented nothing, except a mistake perhaps. A nerdy kid from the ghetto. I was too skinny. Too weak. Even when I played well or ran fast, they hurled insults at me. In San Juan, we'd joked about how I would beat up these *pitucos*, but the reality was so different. They wielded their power carelessly, sometimes unconsciously. They could cut me out with a comment or simply with silence.

"It's time for you to start working," my father announced.

It was my second year at Peruano Británico. I was almost fourteen. In more than a year, I'd never been invited to a classmate's home. Each day I rode the bus from San Juan to San Isidro in silence.

I'd given my father's line of work a lot of thought. I'd examined it under rules of ethics and law. It was wrong. Certainly. But when he told me it was time for me to work, my mind gathered a year of scattered insults and wove them together. I savored those injuries, imagined what a delight it would be to go through one of those boys' houses, to exchange smiles and nods and handshakes. To work there, and then to *steal*. I began to understand my old man, or to think I did. But I wanted to be sure.

"I want to work," I said.

"Of course you do. Every man wants to work."

"Pa, are we going to break into this house?"

He sat back. Frowned. He'd misread me. "Have people been saying things?"

I nodded.

"And what do you think about what they say?" He seemed poised to smile at the slightest hint of approval from me.

"I believe them."

"Well, Chino," he said and stopped.

I wanted to tell him it was all right with me. That those rich fucks could complain to God if they didn't like it. That they could move to Miami and become American. That if they wanted to call me Piraña, then they'd better be good and fucking ready when I came in and repossessed all their treasures.

He ran a finger through his hair and winked. His large black eyes were set close, his mouth was small, comically so, but his broad smile evened everything out, organized the jumble of his features. He kept his black hair meticulously combed back. At rest, he was a caricature of an Indian. In laughter, he was a mestizo Clark Gable. So he laughed and smiled and made that smile the linchpin of his personality. Now he met my gaze, his son—I believed, his only son. "Chino, we're just men who work. You and I both. Crazy things happen in the city." He snapped his fingers and laughed. He hugged me. "Okay?"

The wife had a good eye for color. She had decorated the house herself, she told us. She walked us through the expansive suburban mansion, me, my father, and Felipe, pointing out renovations and design touches: a wall they'd knocked down, leaving only painted beams. "See how this adds space to the room? Gives it another feel?" she asked. The three of us nodded, our eyes wide and observant. There were skylights, balconies, a garden with blossoming trees, but we focused on what could be taken away: a computer, a stereo, even a dishwasher. The husband was an executive at a bank, an old friend of Señor Azcárate. They wanted to remodel the second floor, to add a television room, she said. It wouldn't be that much work, maybe three or four weeks. Some painting. New carpet. A couple of new windows and light fixtures.

I worked on Saturdays, and I saw my father more then than I did at home. During the week, he was mostly gone. His youngest son was still in diapers, and my mother must have known about Carmela by then. When he was home they argued, but I didn't know why. The construction on our house had stalled, the second floor still open air, a thick plastic sheet tied at the corners of three walls. When they were fighting, I retreated there and watched the ridges of the hills draw lines against the sky.

The family we were working for had a son, Andrés, who was in the class above me at Peruano Británico. At his house he ignored me. At school he let it be known that I had crossed the line. I felt the stares, the judgment. By the time he woke up on Saturdays, I had already been working for three or four hours. His weekends, as far as I could tell, took the shape of an extended yawn. I placed tiles in the hallway. He ate cereal. I sanded down corners and measured for the bookshelves we'd be building. He talked on the phone, loud enough for me to hear. "Yeah, Piraña's here. You bet I'm watching my shit, *huevón*." He made no attempt to hide his disdain for me. I listened to him speculate as to which girl would be the first to let him seduce her there. How far she would spread her legs. With a long phone cord dragging behind him, he paraded through the work area, complained of the dust, asked his mother to tell us that the sanding was hurting his ears. He put on a show of power. I bowed my head at the appropriate times and pretended not to hear.

One Saturday, when we were almost done, the entire family was getting ready for a wedding. The mother flitted about, changing her dress three times. The father came in to tell us that we'd have to leave a little early because they all had to go. We were hurrying our work along, trying to finish, when Andrés called out to his mother, "Mami, tell Piraña to stop with the hammering! I can't even think!"

He stepped out into the hallway, wearing a gray wool suit and a red tie, still unknotted. He glared at me.

"What did you call him, Andrés?" his mother said sharply, coming into the room. Her hair was styled in a hard, gelled bob. She stood in front of him, waiting for him to speak.

"Piraña," Andrés muttered.

"What?" she said, surprised, embarrassed. "Why would you call him that?" She turned to me. "Son, what's your name?"

"Oscar, Señora."

"Your mother works with the Azcárates, doesn't she?"

I felt myself turning red. "Yes, Señora."

"And what year are you in?"

"Third, Señora."

Andrés watched this exchange with practiced condescension. In his elegant suit, he was transformed, ready to be photographed for Lima's society pages. He was taller than me, bathed at that moment in superiority, profound and harsh. I wore my work clothes, worn at the knees and splattered with paint.

"Andrés," his mother said, "this is Oscar. This young man is a student at your school. He is friends with Sebastián Azcárate. Now shake his hand and introduce yourself like a gentleman."

His eyes steeled, and his hand too. He held it out.

"Andrés," he said.

"Oscar."

We shook. *No, you were right,* I thought, *Piraña concha tu madre. That's my fucking name.* I glared at him and held his hand, perhaps a moment too long. I squeezed.

"That's enough, boys," his mother said, and they both turned to leave.

"Good afternoon, Señora," I called.

We played to passengers in Santa Anita, Villa Maria, and El Agustino. We rode through Comas, Los Olivos, and Carabayllo. Three days. Lima on display, in all her grandeur, the systems of the city becoming clear to me: her cells, her arteries, her multiple beating hearts. We collected laughs and coins until the money weighed heavy in my suit pocket. I was a secret agent. I saw six people I knew: among them, an ex-girlfriend, two old neighbors from San Juan, and a woman from the university. Even a colleague from the paper. Exactly zero recognized me. I was forgetting myself too, patrolling the city, spying on my own life. I'd never felt this way: on display, but protected from the intruding eyes of strangers and intimates.

I watched the ex-girlfriend chew the nail of her pinky. When we were together, she'd seemed to me the type that would flower, grow into herself, become more attractive each year. But she was twenty-seven now and still not beautiful. I looked her in the eye as she handed me a coin, felt a shock when her finger grazed my open palm. She had no idea who I was.

My old man had paid off the security guard. He'd given us a time and a day. The whole family was out of town. I'd been waiting six months for this. I was a good student and they hated me. I was a good soccer player and they mocked me. I didn't understand a thing about them, or why they were the way they were.

We rode in Felipe's windowless van. They tossed me over the wall. I opened the garage and they backed the van in. The rest was easy. The television, the VCR, the computer, the stereo—each was carried down and packed carefully into the van. We moved nimbly through the dark house, carrying the wares as if they were works of art. And they were. A sleek cordless phone meant thirty soles. A blender, fifteen, if you knew where to sell it. It was so ordered and efficient, it didn't seem like stealing at all.

My father told me once that in Lima anything can be bought and sold. We were walking through the market in San Juan, past the fruit stalls, flies buzzing around the meat and fish. A woman sold clothes piled in high, disordered mounds. Fake Barcelona jerseys. Stolen car parts and bags and watches. An old man stood by his cart of hardware: hammers, pliers, and nails, bent, rusty, unmistakably used. My old man found it pathetic. "Used nails!" he cried out. "For the love of God, are we this poor?"

I did a last run through the house. We were almost done. It was my first time out, my old man's way of saying he trusted me. I wanted in because I trusted him. We were going to be okay. I knew it. We would have money. We would finish the second story of our house, and my mother would be happy again. They would both be happy. I had no idea that he was preparing to leave us.

I lingered at the top of the stairs, looking at the room we'd built. It was really something, even with the gaping hole where the television had been. I was proud of my work. A few steps down the hall, along the tiles I'd laid myself, was Andrés's room. I wasn't looking for anything in particular. We'd already taken his boom box and alarm clock. I turned on the lamp. In the closet there were half a dozen pairs of shoes and button-down shirts in white and blue. I touched them all. I ran my fingers along the rack and found it: his gray wool suit. I'd just pulled it from the closet when my father walked in.

"What the fuck are you doing?" he hissed. "Turn that goddamn light off!"

"I'm sorry," I said. We were in darkness again.

"We're leaving. Put that back," he said. "We can't sell that."

"We could."

"We're in a hurry, Chino. Let's go."

"It's for me," I said.

"This isn't a department store. You don't need that."

He was right. I didn't need it, wouldn't need it. Not until I wore it for my interview at *El Clarín* seven years later. I knew it would take me a year or two to grow into it, if I grew into it at all. It was a dull, shapeless longing, but it was real. "I want this," I said, "for my birthday."

I could barely see him in the purple shadows.

"Your birthday?" my father said. He'd forgotten. "Well then, take it."

I rode around the city in my green-and-white suit and thought about my mother. I put my article in an envelope, sealed it, and dropped it in the mail. I didn't see Villacorta, or check the paper to see if he'd published it. I broke away from Tonio and Jhon, paid them twenty soles for the suit and the shoes and the memories. I thanked them from the very bottom of my new clown heart. And I didn't do their act, or any act. I spent my savings. I put on the polka-dotted suit and stepped into the unwieldy shoes. I painted my face in the dim reflection of the hallway mirror. I placed the red Ping-Pong ball over my nose, felt the tight pull of the rubber band against my hair. And I rode the buses, paying my fare like any other passenger, except that I was unlike any other passenger. I knew I would see her. This was our city, hers and mine. We would meet somewhere beneath Lima's mournful gaze.

I rode to La Victoria, where the corner kids eyed me, wondering if it was worth their trouble to mug a clown. I walked the narrow streets, my shoes flopping on the crumbling sidewalks. I sat on a bench in front of Carmela's house and waited. My black brothers came and went to their schools, to their jobs. They didn't even shoot me a glance. I was part of the architecture. A cop stopped and asked if I was all right.

"Just resting, chief," I said.

Was I from around here?

"I'm Don Hugo's kid."

"Carmela's Hugo?" he asked. Then he left me alone.

Carmela came home carrying dresses, and smiled at me because she smiled at everyone. Her door swung open wide, and from my bench I peered into her world, my mother's new world. And then things came at me in waves: the street, the house. *I haven't seen you since you were this big,* Carmela had said at the hospital. I remembered. When I was six, Don Hugo had taken me to see his mistress. I'd never seen a black person before. I cried and said she looked burnt. She grinned and pinched my cheek. He hit me and told me to be nice to my *tía*. Now I couldn't bring myself to ring the doorbell. I knew she would have been kind, even with me dressed this way. As kind as she was to my mother. She'd answer any of my questions and tell me how she met my father, how she fell for him, the sweet things he'd told her. Carmela and my mother must have spoken of all this already. What revelations did I have for them anyway?

They had worked out the details of their parallel heartbreaks: who had him when, who had him first, who was innocent, who was guilty. And they'd forgiven him, and that was the most astounding thing of all.

Why were you always forgiving him, Ma? He told her everything first—about you, about me, about the work he did and planned to do. He let you swim in darkness, and wonder at the vacant spaces, and ask yourself what mistakes you'd made. And then he left us. And you forgave him, Ma. You forgave him.

After we broke into Andrés's house, the loot was split, but my mother and I saw none of it, except the gray wool suit. The next week I found myself burnishing the lacquered floorboards of another fine home. Another Saturday, and then another. I went on three jobs with my father and his crew. I understand now that money must have been tight. He had four sons to support. We'd just finished a two-week job on a house when Felipe came by with the van. I remember thinking it was strange that they hadn't given the place time to cool. I thought I understood the hustle. I asked my father about it.

"Shut up," he said. "Don't ask questions."

We drove through the dark streets. I sat in the back, felt the van swaying. I had no idea where we were going, but when I got out, I knew immediately where I was. I looked at my father, horrified, expecting some kind of explanation, but he just shrugged. *Crazy things happen in the city.* They boosted me over the wall, into that garden where I'd played as a child. I could see through the glass window, the high bookshelves against the far wall, the elegant leather sofas.

They were too rich and too trusting. Their watchman was asleep in a rickety wooden chair. I opened the garage door from the inside and the man woke with a start. My father stepped in and broke his jaw. Felipe dragged him into the garden and tied him to a tree. The watchman sat there, blindfolded and gagged and bleeding, while we disassembled the house. Their possessions were so familiar it was like stealing from myself.

It was terrifying and logical: the riskiest hit of all. I led Felipe and my father around the house like a tour guide: don't forget the microwave and the blender my mother loves so much. And, in here, the clock and the old engineer's nifty calculator and the television with its remote control. There was something beautiful in our silent artistry. Everyone would be a suspect. The gardener, my mother, my father, me. Whichever members of the crew had worked on the house. And the watchman tied to the tree, bleeding into a rag.

The van was full. It was time to go. The watchman's chin was slumped into his chest, his breathing heavy. I felt the conviction that he too was one of us, and it disgusted me. It could have been anything: a stray light that shone on him or a spasm in his face that made me think he was smiling. I kicked him. He snapped to attention, seeing only his blindfold. He struggled against the tree. I hocked something viscous and unclean on his forehead. *The color of money.*

My father called me, and we disappeared.

She left Carmela's and I followed her. She got on the bus at Manco Capac. She wore her uniform, as clean and as white as a high summer cloud. She didn't notice me behind her, sat across from me innocently, not even looking in my direction. I closed my eyes, felt the rumble of the bus along the potholed avenue. The ticket collector sang the route: La Victoria, San Borja! La Victoria, San Borja! Between the standing passengers, I could still catch glimpses of her. No one sat in the empty seat beside me. Then she stood. She got off, and I followed.

I knew the way, of course, to my Saturday home, where I once kept my mother company and did my homework on the garden terrace. The space my father and I had violated, nearly sacrificing her livelihood. But she had always been safe there. And, worse, I had too. They'd welcomed me into their looted house, consoled me when I cried. *You're too old for that, Chino. Look, they didn't steal the books.* The old engineer with his generous heart, trying to make me feel better.

I trailed a half block behind her now, an expert in my clumsy green shoes. She walked along the sidewalk and I tracked her, marching down the very center of an empty street. "Ma!" I shouted. "Ma!" She half-turned, and then sped up at the sight of me. I rushed to keep pace with her. "Ma!" I shouted again. "Ma, it's Oscar! It's Chino!"

She stopped beneath a flowering tree and stepped out into the street. *"Hijo?"* she said. "Is that you?"

I hadn't seen her since the *velorio*. I had left her to bury the old man without me. She had held his hand and watched him die. She had put him in the earth and covered him.

"It's me, Ma."

"Chino!" she cried. "You scared me!"

"I'm sorry, Ma."

"Your nose, Chino?"

I pulled off my red nose, let it drop to the ground.

"And your shoes? What's all this?"

I stepped out of the clown shoes and kicked them toward the sidewalk. "I'm writing a story, Ma. For the paper."

She nodded, not understanding.

"I'm sorry," I repeated.

"Where have you been, Chino?"

"Here and there," I said. I took off my wig. "I'm here now."

She took me in her arms and stroked my hair. She kissed my forehead and wiped the paint from my cheeks. "Are you all right?"

"I've been to Carmela's, but I didn't knock."

"You should have," she said. "Will you?"

"I don't know," I said. "Did he ask about me?"

It was a travesty, my wanting to know, but I did. She held me tighter. My face paint was running, coming off in white streaks on the sleeve of my suit. "He missed you, Chino," she said.

I felt the warm, salty wet of her cheek against mine. It felt good to be held.

"I missed you too," my mother said.

"I won't leave you," I cried. But a shiver passed over me. I knew in my heart that the clown was lying.

third avenue suicide

They'd been living in the apartment for ten days when David was first asked to disappear. This was the arrangement, what they'd agreed upon, and he would do so without complaint. His things were put away, hidden in the corners of the closet, or under the bed, or in the bottom drawer where Reena's mother was unlikely to look. His razor, his boxer shorts, his guitar, his cameras. "Your man things," Reena said, joking. He liked the way she said it. David kissed her and walked out of the apartment and into the street. The August heat had broken, and the breezy afternoon intimated the coming fall. I'm a good boyfriend, David told himself. It was no sacrifice at all. He loved her. He sat on the curb across the street from their building, smoking cigarettes and watching for Mrs. Shah.

He'd seen Reena's mother in pictures many times and once in person at Reena's dance performance the previous spring. Mrs. Shah didn't know Reena had a boyfriend. She didn't know they'd been dating for two years, or that they'd just moved in together. And she could not know. These were the rules of the relationship, Reena said. When I'm ready, I'll tell her.

Her father had not known either. He'd passed away in April, not knowing.

When you're ready, David said, nodding. He wanted to be patient. Not to pressure her.

Now he waited and wondered exactly how long he would have to be outdoors. A breeze carried some candy wrappers toward the park at the top of the hill. Some older men stood on the corner, thumbing through a newspaper they'd laid out on the hood of a parked car. One of them nodded at David. A game of baseball was under way in the middle of the street. A spindly-legged kid swung wildly at a tennis ball, launching fly balls high into the air.

David bought a paper at the bodega and read the sports. He smoked two cigarettes. The men dispersed and regrouped on another corner, caressing beer bottles in brown paper bags. The call from the Yankees game spilled out of a car stereo. David had forgotten to watch for Reena's mother. He'd missed her emerging from the train station, or toddling up the hill. Instead, he read the paper cover to cover, news that bored him thoroughly, as an hour passed, and most of another. He walked around the block and sat down again. The afternoon edged toward dusk, and suddenly there was Reena in front of him, grinning. "She's gone," Reena said. "Are you coming up?"

"What'd she say?" David asked.

"Nothing really."

David checked at his watch. "In two hours?"

"Well . . ."

"Did she like the place?"

"She said it was dark."

He nodded. It *was* dark. "Foggy," he said, shaking his head.

"We'll go crazy in there." With arching eyebrows, David signified crazy. Reena laughed.

The day they rented the apartment had been sunny and clear, a washed-out and white afternoon. It fooled them: the tiny space seemed, that morning, endearingly intimate and warm. They'd spent more than a week unpacking, cleaning, and painting; not once had it approached the bright golden light of that first day. "Indifferent to light," was how Reena described the apartment. Outside, the quality of the sun changed: shadows glancing at various angles, transforming the city as the day grew older. But inside their space, the walls stayed a dull white and nothing glowed and nothing shone. A uniform blue evoked midwinter. It was, they decided, the city's darkest nonbasement apartment.

Now David held his hands out. Reena pulled him up. "She didn't even look in the closets. Or under the bed. You're off the hook." She bit her lip and tucked a loose strand of black hair behind her ear. "She did ask me if I was seeing anyone."

"And? What'd you tell her?"

"That me and my hoodrat boyfriend make love every night on the fire escape."

Reena touched his cheek, and David felt the muscles of his face contract into a smile. Over her shoulder, he could see the older men watching them.

"Underneath the stars. How romantic."

"Without protection," she whispered.

"Mongrel babies."

"Half-breeds.

"The best kind," he said. Her breath tickled his ear. He buried his head between her neck and shoulder, felt her tighten when he bit her earlobe. He kissed her neck until Reena laughed.

"She told me there are Web sites for Indians now," Reena said. "Web sites? Can you imagine?"

"How primitive modern." David frowned and pulled away. "She's not giving up then."

"Nope."

He shook his head and realized he was expecting something. It had been two hours. He felt the need to be thanked. They were quiet for a moment. On the sidewalk, the breeze turned the newspaper's crumpled pages.

"She brought us fruit," Reena said finally.

"Ooohh."

"Don't be an ass." She twirled a lock of black hair around her finger and then took his hand.

"Do you think she'll come around much?"

"Probably not." Reena kissed him. They crossed the street toward their apartment.

But she did come around, once the next week, and twice the week after that. David soon understood exactly what was in store. Reena lived in the apartment, he visited there. All the bills were in her name. David had bought a cell phone, since he was prohibited from answering the land line. It was the number Reena's mother called. The first weeks of September, there was still little to be done at work, and so often he was home early, only to be displaced by Reena's mother. He got to know the neighborhood during these periods of exile. He walked up to Riverside Park, where the Mexicans played volleyball beneath the leafy shade of the oak trees. He had coffee at La Floridita and pretended to play Lotto with those stubby yellow pencils. He window-shopped on 125th, looked disinterestedly at bright

Timberland boots engineered like SUVs, and baby blue FUBU jogging suits selling for two bills. But always before he left, David waited for Mrs. Shah and tried to intercept her. He'd seen Reena's mother three times now, walking slowly up the hill from the train station, bearing gifts: a grocery bag full of apples, a duffel packed with bath towels, and once, an electric juicer, brand-new and still in the box. Afterward, when he came home and Reena showed off what her mother had brought them, David warily pointed out that these gifts, no matter how thoughtful, were not for them. They were for her. In any case, he saw Mrs. Shah before Reena did, saw her struggling up the hill with heavy bags, arms clasped around a package, and he never offered to help, though this went against every impulse he had, everything he had ever been taught. Instead he walked by, smiling generously. His idea was to pass her each and every time she came until she noticed him.

"She won't, you know," Reena said when he told her his plan. They were unpacking a bag full of sweaters that Mrs. Shah had brought, though the cold was still weeks away.

"She could."

"Sure. She *could*. But she won't."

"I'll bump into her," David said. "I'll help her carry her bags up the hill."

Reena groaned.

"I'm playing," David said.

"Well, don't. Me living alone is a big deal to her. Everything is. You know she wanted me to move home. Anything more is too much," Reena said. "She'd *die*."

The last syllable hung there, and David believed none of it. "That's *not* how people die," he said. David held a stack of sweaters—ugly sweaters—in his hands, was poised to stash them away on a top shelf in the closet. Instead he tossed them on the bed. "No one dies 'cause their daughter's got a boyfriend."

She glared at him. "Don't talk like that," she said curtly. "You don't know how people die." Her old man had been out running, on a doctor's suggestion that he get more exercise. He'd been ailing for years but, it seemed, had turned a corner. Then, heart attack.

Reena turned on a lamp. She squinted. They'd declared the dark their enemy, painted the walls a shade of red David called "the color of action." Hundred-watt bulbs in three lamps. They gave the impression of a room on fire.

"I'm sorry . . ." David trailed off. "I feel like I'm sneaking around," he said, turning on the stereo. The wired voice of a radio DJ filled the room.

"You *are* sneaking around. Jesus. We both are. My mother wants to marry me off to some dentist. My wedding was all they ever talked about. She's checking the fucking Internet." Reena picked up the sweaters and, on the tips of her toes, tossed them up on the top shelf. Her breasts bounced once as she jumped. Reena turned to face David, who'd taken a seat by the desk. "I lie to her every day. You think this is a cakewalk for me?"

"I didn't say that."

"They're—*She's* not going to stop until I'm Mrs. Patel or Mrs. Singh or Mrs. Kumar. Mrs. Nice Indian Boy."

"And?" he said.

Reena sighed. Her lips were pursed and tight. "You want me to tell her? Are you ready for that?" she asked. "You know what would happen?"

David stared at her black eyes. She was beautiful, too beautiful for him. Once, she hadn't been so afraid. He turned away from her. "Whatever," he muttered, grateful, suddenly, for all the diffuse meanings of that word.

"Do you know how fucked up it would be?"

"You've told me."

"She's alone now." Reena stepped toward him. "I'm what she has." She softened. "Don't make this your problem," she said. "Please. You don't want it."

David sighed. "It's just fucked up."

"It is. Of course it is."

"Come here," he said and made room for her on his lap. "Who likes fucked up?" David asked.

"No one," Reena said.

They had been living in the city's darkest studio apartment for two months when Reena awoke one morning, tired. She'd had the flu or something, and was taking too long to get over it. Weeks and weeks of fighting her own body, of OJ and vitamins and yoga in the mornings to work out the stiffness. She dragged herself to the shower, pulled on her clothes with cumbrous movements, and smiled feebly at David as she got ready for work. He sat up in bed and massaged her shoulders. A radio newscaster announced all the day's tragedies. David didn't have to be at the center until ten and, once there, rarely did any real work before eleven. Reena seemed beat, he thought, and he told her so. She confessed that she had felt even more tired the last couple of days. He rose and, before she left, promised he'd call her from work, when he got a free moment.

"Is there another kind at your fake-ass job?" Reena said, laughing.

The room was red and bright. The lamps were on. "I like my

free moments. I like my fake-ass job," he said, which was mostly true. David blew her a kiss. "Feel better," he called out.

He didn't think much of it at work. It was late October, and the center was dressed in the obligatory Halloween orange and black. David spent the morning sending e-mails. He answered a couple of phone calls about tutoring. A kid he knew from Stanley Isaacs Houses came in and asked to borrow some money. He and another counselor talked about how pathetic the Knicks would be that year. He watched a trashy Spanish talk show with a roomful of seniors. He ate lunch alone on the benches beneath the project shadows, blew smoke rings and watched the cars drive up Third Avenue.

It was a quarter to seven before he got home. Reena was already there. The apartment smelled awful. Reena looked awful. The bathroom door was open and the light was on. The room glowed a sickly yellow and orange hue. She sat up in bed when he came in. "Hey, babe," Reena said in a tired voice.

"You all right? What's going on?"

She wasn't feeling well, she'd had to come home.

"You should've called me at the center," David said.

"I thought you were going to call me."

David winced.

"I just came home and fell asleep anyway," Reena said, shrugging. "Well, slept and threw up a little. I ate some soup. That must be it."

He made her tea, and Reena said she was feeling better, but all night she kept waking up and stumbling to the bathroom. She threw up four times. It was nearly daybreak when she and David admitted that they weren't going to get any sleep. The pungent smell of vomit hung in the small apartment like a toxic cloud.

The cab ride to the emergency room reminded David of everything he hated about the city. A weak dawn sun cast no shadows. Dogs and people picked through piles of trash. Reena slumped into his lap, and he stroked her hair. She was feverish. It occurred to David that Reena might be pregnant. He felt his stomach sink. Her eyes were closed and they were still five blocks from the hospital. The idea of it spread until he could feel fear humming in the very tips of his fingers. He didn't mention it to her.

In the waiting room, Reena called her mother on David's cell phone. David held her hand as she spoke, could feel in her pulse the effort she was making to sound stronger than she was. *Tik,* she said, which was the only Hindi word he knew. It meant okay. The conversation was brief. Mrs. Shah was coming, of course.

For a moment, David allowed himself to consider the possibility that Reena was really ill. There they were together, hands clasped, in the waiting room of a public hospital. Her mother would come. He would be courteous. Responsible. Explain things—*I am the boyfriend*—and everything else: Reena's last few weeks, how tired she seemed and stiff, and what he'd observed from watching her, being with her, and loving her, every day in the apartment they'd shared since August.

"I love you, babe," David said.

Reena nodded.

"Should I leave?" he asked, hopefully.

She lay her head against his right shoulder instead. He put his arm around her and rubbed her temple with his thumb. He listened to the soft rhythm of her breathing.

"Not yet," Reena said finally. "In a while."

His hand stopped moving of its own accord. David felt a

heat in his chest, a sensation so unpleasant he wondered for a moment if whatever Reena had was contagious. Mrs. Shah was on her way from Englewood, just across the George Washington Bridge. It would be twenty minutes more, maybe twenty-five. Another half hour before he was displaced, and until then he could rub her head and soothe her and then he would have to go. Or he could leave now. He felt icy and useless. He eased her head off his shoulder. "How do you feel?" he asked.

"Everything hurts." Her face drooped into a sad frown. Reena held her hand out, and for a moment, it hung there between them. She looked pitiful. He took her hand in his and massaged it. He pulled it to his lips and kissed the third knuckle. He stood to leave.

"Will you clean up the place?" Reena asked. "In case my mom wants to take me back there?"

David said he would.

All alone in the apartment, David appreciated its darkness. He sprawled out on the bed and left the lamps off. The faucet dripped. It would be such a childish gesture, but somehow satisfying: to leave a clue. Something undeniably his. His basketball, scuffed and bruised on the Riverside courts; or his camera, which he'd used to take pictures of Reena at her last dance performance. He got up and pulled the curtain, the anemic midmorning light filtered in through the window. He thumbed through a stack of photographs on the desk and found the one shot he loved of Reena in her mustard-colored sari, gold earrings and glittering bracelets on her wrists and on her ankles above her graceful, bare feet. She was gleaming and young. Her parents were there. How close he had been to them, as if he could have stepped out of the crowd and into their world, and offered his hand: Mr. Shah. Mrs. Shah. How simple it would have been.

Her father had died a few weeks later. Then Reena had started working at a lab uptown and studying full-time. She had dropped her dance classes altogether.

David showered and put away his things. On his knees, he cleaned the bathroom. He left a fine mist of aerosol disinfectant floating in the air, a lemony medicinal scent that stung the inside of his throat. He left and locked the door.

By mid-December, she'd been to three doctors. Lyme disease, said the first. The second mentioned lupus, but said he couldn't be certain. The third, whom Reena chose to believe for the calm and reassuring manner in which he spoke, diagnosed early-onset arthritis. It was comforting, she told David, to have a diagnosis, a name to give her symptoms. She'd quit her job. Most days she wanted to lie in bed. Her knees hurt. Her elbows. The individual joints of her fingers. On the worst days, she described steel rods running the length of her legs, unbendable knees, the stiffness of a frozen cadaver. The doctor said it would pass, but Reena told David that sometimes she felt she was dying. I'm too young for this, she said.

Her mother came nearly every day now, and David wondered, in his more selfish moments, what was worse: a sick girlfriend or her overbearing mother exiling you to the streets. Reena and David hadn't made love since before the trip to the emergency room. She was always tired, or looked so ill and unhappy that he was afraid touching her might be interpreted as an assault. Her mother came and stayed late, sometimes till eight or nine. She cried with her daughter and told Reena that someone had cursed them. She burned incense and herbs with such overpowering odors that the neighbors complained. They prayed together while David waited outside, or at La Floridita, brooding, for Reena to call him on his cell phone so he could come home. He still waited for Mrs. Shah, watching for her unsure steps as she came down the escalator from the train. Each time, Mrs. Shah turned uncertainly toward 125th Street, or looked down Broadway, a pause as if lost, before heading up toward the apartment.

David steadfastly refused to abandon his project. He wanted more than ever to crack into Mrs. Shah's world. There was something in her that he recognized: the way she walked, the little regard she had for the neighborhood, or for the particulars of the street, or for him, planted somewhere along her short path from train to apartment. That invisibility is not me, he reasoned. It is her. He didn't know what part of India Reena's family was from, but it was, he imagined, nothing like this. It was not squat gray buildings. It was not the south edge of Harlem. It was not kids in oversize black jackets huddled on corners, or the boom-bip of a snare drum escaping from the window of a Jeep. It was not lazy Spanish in bodegas, or Goya beans, or storefront windows that bathed cell phones in green neon light. It was not Malian women standing by the train, offering to braid hair with nimble fingers. Wherever Mrs. Shah was from had none of these things. And so, Mrs. Shah could walk through it, as if in a fog, and not see it, and not care; and David could smile and nod a hundred times, and never be seen. Her husband was dead. Reena was the only real person in her city.

The first snow fell and melted into black-brown sludge, piling icy and unclean in the city's gutters. On a Thursday afternoon, David waited for Mrs. Shah. He sat on the front step of the building, holding a stack of books and folders full of papers. The director had assigned social work readings for an upcoming staff development day. Upstairs, Reena was yellow and sick, drowsy with pills. She complained that the medicine was making her gain weight. David pretended not to have noticed.

The block was quiet, in its winter grays. At the bottom of the hill, Mrs. Shah emerged from the train station. David gathered his things and made his way down the hill to meet her. To walk by her. He would make eye contact this time. He would nod. He would offer to carry her bag for her. The sidewalk was slippery. David wiggled his toes inside his boots. And Mrs. Shah trudged slowly up the block, arms empty, wearing a grim, determined expression, as if fighting the cold. These were sad visits. She was wrapped in a black wool coat, her head covered by a bright orange scarf. She looked straight ahead.

Halfway down the block, David felt the helplessness of that moment just before one is ignored. It stung. Reena, he felt certain, would kill him for what he was about to do, but, in any case, it was done: a few feet in front of Reena's mother, David pretended to stumble and then, despite himself, he did. He lost his balance on the slick pavement. His books and papers spilled everywhere. He slid back until he was down, ass on the cold, wet sidewalk, Mrs. Shah standing over him. He was out of breath. He looked her in the eye.

"Young man," Mrs. Shah said, with a look of surprise and worry, "are you all right?"

He'd crossed some line. She seemed genuinely concerned, more than simply polite. She would remember his face. She looked as he imagined Reena's mother should: with Reena's deep brown eyes, her full lips, her delicate nose. Mrs. Shah was a little darker than her daughter, who was a bit darker than David. She smiled kindly, the lines on her face deeper and more noticeable than when he had last seen her. She had aged in these months, carrying the burden of her daughter's illness.

Mrs. Shah asked again, "Are you all right?" She offered him a hand.

"Me? Oh yes," David said. "*Tik*. I'm fine."

"Sorry?"

"*Tik*," he repeated. He hadn't expected to fall. He'd only wanted to drop the books. He felt his palms sweating on the inside of his gloves. "I'm fine."

By the look of befuddlement on Mrs. Shah's face, David knew he had gone too far. She would mention it to Reena. *Tik*. It would become a question. She would want to know what was going on. "Thank you," David said as Reena's mother passed him a book. She stood there, watching him as he stacked his things on the sidewalk.

"Thank you," he said again, then he took his books and papers under his arm and barreled down the hill toward the train.

When they met and started dating, Reena often described the situation ironically: a bind, she said, a circumstance. *A context*. They talked for hours and hurt themselves laughing. Her situation didn't change or go away; they simply chose to ignore it. There was no logic to it, no forward thinking: they had no other choice.

Fathers are worse, Reena had said. They're rock, unmovable stone, bulwarks of tradition. Fathers are more protective of daughters, less understanding, have more invested in the idea of good marriages. Mothers want sons so they can browbeat their daughters-in-law one day, the way they themselves were tormented by their mothers-in-law years before. In fact, everyone wants sons. Daughters: they should marry well and early, avoiding the Western problems of dating, boyfriends, and sex. Prospective husbands: caste matters less than profession. Doctors, engineers, lawyers, in that order. Reena claimed not to know which caste her parents were from. She said it exactly that way, with those words—*my parents are from*—because she didn't belong to any caste at all. She was American. A *Desi*, but still American. I'm both, she said. I was raised this way. They would find her a husband. It wasn't foreign or strange. It simply was.

"But," she said to David once, "you could almost pass, you know? You're vaguely *something*."

Ideas were being kicked around, ways to circumvent the *context*. David raised an eyebrow. "Pass as?"

"They're your color in the north. With green eyes. Kashmiri. I've seen it." Reena smiled mischievously. "Time to learn you some Punjabi, babe. Teach you to dance Bhangra."

"And become an engineer."

"Yep. Social work won't do."

"And I gotta rock more gold."

"And we should clean that Spanish off you."

They'd been dating for four and a half months when she announced she would try her mother. It surprised him. And it might have surprised her to know that, though he was touched, the first question that crossed his mind was, What will this require of me? He asked her carefully, not wanting to dissuade her, and not at all sure what any of it meant. "Why me?" he said.

"Because I love you," she answered.

Her father he had a picture of: not well, grumpy in the face of prolonged illness, furrowed brow, deep-set eyes. Probably hated white people more than he hated blacks. At best, indifferent to Spanish folks. Dissatisfied. Nostalgic. David's first, unspoken question grew specifically out of Reena's description of her father. The rust-red color of his angry face. How he would disown her. Curse her. Die. Disruptions to the tranquility of the *context* were described in terms of international crisis areas, civil wars. A family torn asunder, a daughter abandoned, an unsuspecting boyfriend wondering what the hell happened.

Mrs. Shah was his ally against Reena's father. She was reason, and reason would prevail. Mrs. Shah would recognize that he loved her daughter. She would be his foot in the door. That Reena would risk telling her mother anything at all touched David. It was Reena's leap of faith.

"I like a boy," she told her mother.

And this is what Mrs. Shah said, according to Reena: "No, you don't. Your father is sick. It's your last semester. You're going to have to find a job. How can you think about a boy?"

Reena laughed when she told him, recounting the whole incident with an amused smile. Cluelessness. Foreignness. Her poor mother. David felt disappointment and relief in equal parts. He bristled at the notion of being called a "boy" by both his girlfriend and her mother. Reena was something less than a woman if she had to ask permission to see him. On the other hand, it was a war that she probably only wanted to fight once: was he worth it? Reena wouldn't want to fight alone. War implied all kinds of commitments.

In any case, it was done. There would be no going public. The *context* would not be disturbed. And so they forgot it when they could, let themselves fall in love, and found those amnesiac moments to be their best.

"Leave," Reena said. "Please."

It was February. December had passed, and January, and Reena had stayed sick. The doctors said she'd be better by spring. They told her optimistically that she'd be dancing again in no time at all. Now her mother was coming. Had called twenty minutes before, was on her way. David should have left already. His usual seat at La Floridita was waiting for him, and the curly-haired waitress who would bring him coffee and a Lotto ticket and a stubby yellow pencil. The slick city sidewalks. The rumble of a passing train. All the routines of disappearance were waiting for him out in the streets. But he felt something heavy in him, something leaden and stiff. Something arthritic. Cataleptic. David sat at the desk. The red walls sometimes unnerved him, but today he felt their heat.

"It's cold out," he offered.

"David."

"What?" he said blankly.

"You're stressing me out," Reena said. "Go get a cup of coffee. Do you need money? Here, take some money." She offered him a few rumpled bills.

"You don't have a job."

Scowling, she let the money slip from fingers. "What are you trying to do? Are you trying to make this difficult?"

"No."

"Then? Are you going to wait until she buzzes? Till she knocks?"

"I don't know," he said.

"I'm sick, goddamn it, I'm sick!"

The picture he'd left had made no impact. Reena's mother hadn't asked who took it. Or why it was in black-and-white. David had stalked his girlfriend and her parents at Union Square, taking black-and-white pictures that were not quite beautiful. Reena hadn't even noticed it on the desk. Mrs. Shah had said only how handsome Reena's father had looked that day.

It was subtle. But falling on his ass in front of Mrs. Shah? Nothing. Reena's mother had commented on it and forgotten. Found it funny. *Tik*. That was all. A week after he'd tumbled to the frozen sidewalk, Mrs. Shah had walked right by him without so much as a glance.

Since then, he'd learned two new words that he hadn't yet had the chance to say:

Namaste. Hello.

Amah. Mother.

If he still wanted to be found, he'd have to stop her on the street. Catch her on the stairs walking up to the apartment. Look into her brown eyes and speak in complete Hindi sentences:

Hello, mother. I am a wealthy Punjabi engineer looking for an American-born Desi to warm my bed. For marriage and dowry, and perhaps for love. My mother will not mistreat your daughter after the wedding. I promise you this, Mrs. Shah.

Would that be enough?

Mrs. Shah, I am David. My parents are Peruvian. I work in the projects. Your daughter and I, we live together. We used to make love on the fire escape. I have cleaned up her vomit. I have watched her get sick. Sometimes, I think I still love her, but I'm tired.

His jacket landed on his lap, followed by his scarf, and then his gloves. He looked up at Reena, tired and sad against the red walls. She sat on the edge of the bed. "You want your sweatshirt too?"

"Yeah," David said.

She tossed him his hoodie. "We can't talk about this now," Reena said.

"I know."

"Later?"

"Sure," he said, nodding.

Her face disappeared into her hands. She was taking a dozen pills a day. Each Friday, the doctors gave her a shot in the thigh with a long needle. He put on his sweatshirt, and then his jacket. He took his key off the hook by the door, his knit cap from on top of the dresser. It was cold out. He put on his gloves, left hand first. The room was bright and warm and red.

lima, peru, july 28, 1979

There were ten of us and we shared a single name: compañero. Except me. They called me Pintor. Together we formed an uncertain circle around a dead dog, under the dim lights just off the plaza. Everything was cloaked in fog. Our first revolutionary act, announcing ourselves to the nation. We strung up dogs from all the street lamps, covered them with terse and angry slogans, Die Capitalist Dogs and such; leaving the beasts there for the people to see how fanatical we could be. It is clear now that we didn't scare anyone so much as we disturbed them and convinced them of our peculiar mania, our worship of frivolous violence. Fear would come later. Killing street dogs in the bleak gray hours before sunrise, the morning of Independence Day, July 28, 1979. Decent people slept, but we made war, fashioned it with our hands, our knives, and our sweat. Everything was going well until we ran out of black dogs.

One of the *compañeros* had directed that all the dogs were to be black, and we were in no position to question these things. An aesthetic decision, not a practical one. Lima has a nearly infinite supply of mutts, but not all of them are black. By two o'clock, we were slopping black paint on beige, brown, and white mutts, all squirming away the last of their breaths, fur tinged with red.

Given my erstwhile talents with the brush, I was charged with painting the not-quite-black ones. We had one there: dead, split open, its viscera slipping onto the pavement. We were tired, trying to decide if this mutt's particular shade of brown was dark enough to pass for black. I don't recall many strong opinions on the matter. The narcotic effects of action were drifting away, leaving us with a bleeding animal, dead, a shade too light.

I didn't care what color the dog was.

Just as we were coming to a consensus that we would paint the dead mutt we had at our feet—just then I saw it: from the corner of my eye, darting down an alleyway, a black dog. It was spectacularly black, completely black, and before I knew it, I found myself racing down the cobblestones after it. I dropped the paintbrush one of my *compañeros* had handed me. They called after me, "Pintor!" but I was gone.

Enraged, I chased after the black animal, hoping to kill it, bring it back, string it up. That night, the way things were going, I wanted, more than anything, for my actions to make sense. I was tired of painting.

You should know the homeless dogs of Lima inhabit a higher plane of ruthlessness. They own the alleys, they are thieves of the colonial city, undressing trash heaps, urinating in cobblestone corners, always with an eye open. They're witnesses to murders, robberies, shakedowns; they hustle through the streets with self-assurance, with a confidence that comes from knowing they don't have to eat every day to live. That night we ran all over the plaza, butchering them, in awe of their treachery, raw and golden.

I knew how many cigarettes I smoked each day, and I knew

how little I ran except when chasing a soccer ball now and then if a game came up, and I knew that there was little chance of catching it and—I'll admit—it angered me to know that a dog might outdo me, and so I resolved that it would not. We ran. It surged ahead. I followed along the narrows of central Lima, beneath her ragged and decaying balconies, past her boarded buildings, her cloistered doorways, her shadows. I wanted the mutt dead. I ran with cruelty in my chest, like a drug pushing me faster, and then my leg buckled and I sputtered to a stop. I was blocks away from the plaza, in the grassy median of a broad, silent avenue lined with anemic palm trees, dizzy, lungs gasping for air. The poor dog slowed on the far sidewalk and turned to look at me, standing only a few feet away, panting, its head turned quizzically to one side, a look I've seen before, from family, from friends, or even from women unfortunate enough to love me, the look of those who wonder at me, who expect things and are eventually disappointed.

You should know that I felt nothing for the dog other than steely blue-black hatred. I was cold and angry. Hurt by too many German philosophers in translation. Wounded by watching my father go blind beneath great swaths of leather, bending and manipulating each until, like magic, a belt, or a saddle, or a soccer ball appeared. Frustrated by an absurd evening spent killing and painting for the revolution. I hated the dog. In the Arequipa of my youth, a street mutt had slept in our doorway once in a while, and mostly I had ignored it, had not petted it, but had watched it scratch itself or lick its own testicles and had never been stirred. I have loved many things, many people, but I felt no warmth toward this beast. Instead I envisioned there were stages of death, degrees of it, a descending staircase, and I wanted with all my heart to see this mutt, with its matted black fur, resting at the bottom. I called it and held my hand out. I sucked my teeth and coaxed it to me.

And it came. With a pit-pat of paws on the concrete, it crossed the avenue, as if it were coming home, as if it were somewhere else entirely, not in the midst of war. It was a beautiful dog, an innocent dog. It had a shiny black coat. It had been playing a game. Still, I felt anger toward it—for making me run, for each drop of sweat, for the heavy beating of my heart. I petted it for a moment, then grasped it by the nape of its neck, plunged the knife through its black fur, and twisted.

At that last moment, the dog struggled mightily, growling, lunging, but I held on and it did not bite me, but fell to the ground in a heap, blood gathering in a pool beneath its wound.

It groaned sadly, helplessly. I admired it as it bled: its strong white teeth, its muscular hind legs. It panted and heaved. I might have stayed there all night if not for a flash of light and gruff voice that called out. It was a police officer and he had a gun.

In Arequipa, I chiseled decorations on the saddles my father crafted each year for the parades. I helped him dye the leathers, and took the hammer and the small wedge and banged and hit and bled until each was beautiful. This is how I was raised: my father and I in the workshop, the intoxicating smell of the cured leather, the tools, each with its purpose and mythology. He taught me the meticulous process as his eyesight abandoned him. By the time I had mastered it, he was too blind to see my work. My mother would tell him, "The boy is learning," and he glowed.

I dressed impeccably in my gray and white school uniform, and always did more than was expected of me. I placed first in my class, and took the university entrance exam at age seventeen. I was accepted to the university in Lima. My head was shaved, my father danced happily, and my mother cried, knowing I would soon leave her. Lima was known then for swallowing lives, drawing people from their ancestral homes, enveloping us in her concrete and noise. I became one of those people. I saw the city and felt its chaos and its energy; I couldn't go home.

I have lived through Lima's turbulent adolescence and her unbounded growth. She is mine now. I am not afraid of her, even as I am no longer in love with her. At the university I studied philosophy and then transferred to fine arts to study painting. I made angry canvases of red and black, with terrorized faces hidden beneath swaths of bold color. I painted in Rimac, just across the dirty river, in a small room with a window that looked out at the graceful contour of the colonial city. It was often cloudy, and my elderly landlady, Doña Alejandra, liked to let herself into my room to look at my work. I came upon her there, wrapped in my threadbare blanket, asleep in my chair, her chest rising in shallow breaths, on one of the handful of sunny days that I remember. Her own room had no windows.

I caught the eye of some people with a painting I exhibited at the university: a portrait of a man, eyes averted, his mouth squeezed in a tight grimace, gripping a hammer in his right hand, poised to nail a stake square into the flat of his left palm. He was blue and brown geometry against a red background. He was my father.

In the cafeteria, students stood on tables to denounce the dictator and his cronies. Slogans appeared on brick walls and were whitewashed by timid workers, only to appear again. We knew the struggle would come. It was the same all over the country. Many left school to prepare for the coming war.

My father's blindness had hurt me. I longed to show him what I had accomplished. On my last visit home, in our small anteroom, I repainted my canvases with words, slowly, and only for him. He gazed blankly at the walls. I talked him through years of my canvases but never cracked the austere dark of his blindness. He nodded, told me he understood, but I knew I had failed him.

I returned from Arequipa and made my decision. I left the university for the last time, only three months before I was to receive my degree in the fine arts. Instead I traveled to the countryside to study explosives with my *compañeros*.

If I were still a painter, I could show you some truths about this place: the children, cold and hungry, lining up each morning at the well, carrying water back to their families. Five kilometers. Seven kilometers. Nine. The endless bus rides across the city, when a young man in an ill-fitting suit steps aboard to recite poetry and sell Chiclets. "It's not charity I am asking for," he shouts over the rattle of a dying bus. "I am selling a poem to ease your commute!" The passengers look down and away.

In 1970, a town disappeared beneath the Andes. An earthquake. Then a landslide. Not a village but a town. Yungay. It was a Sunday afternoon; my father and I listened to the World Cup live from Mexico City, Peru playing Argentina to a respectable draw, when the room shook, vaguely. And then the news came slowly; filtered, like all things in Peru, from the provinces to Lima, and then back out again to all the far-flung corners of our make-believe nation. We were aware that something unspeakable had occurred, but could not name it just yet. The earth had spilled upon itself, an angry sea of mud and rock, drowning thousands. Only some of the children were spared. A traveling circus had set up camp at the higher end of the valley. There were clowns in colorful hats and children laughing as their parents were buried.

In Arequipa, to the south, we had scarcely felt the earthquake at all: a vase slipping off a windowsill, a picture hanging askew, a dog barking.

If I were still a painter, I would set up a canvas on that barren spot where that town once stood, select my truest colors, and show you that life can disappear just like that. "And what is this, Pintor?" you might ask, pointing to the ochre, purple, orange, and gray.

Ten thousand graves; can't you see them?

When I was a painter, I would stroll through the city, eyes wide open. On my way home each afternoon, I passed the roadside mechanics standing along the avenue at the end of a day's work. Stained oily black from head to toe, they were the fiercest angels, the city's living dead. Lima was full of those worn down by living. I rushed home, reeling, sketching on napkins, papers, on my skin, all that I had seen so it would not go unrecorded. Everything meant something, hinted at an as-yet-unasked, un-dreamed-of question. There were no answers that convinced me. I painted toward those questions—a cinder block resting in an abandoned parking lot, a dented fender reflecting the streets—sometimes for a day or two or even three, catnapping in the corner of my room just as my landlady Doña Alejandra had once. I awoke well before dawn, awash in the metallic odors of paint and sweat and hunger, and I forgot my body almost completely.

I have found that sensation a few times since: lost in the tangle of vines, in the jungles of northern Peru, running from an ambush; setting a bomb in the bitter cold of the sierra beneath a concrete bridge. But like a drug, each time the adrenaline rush is less powerful, and each culminating boom means less and less.

I have not painted since that night of the dogs. Not a stroke of black or red, not animal or canvas.

And I will not paint again.

Only the walls of my cell—if they catch me—a shade recalling sky, so my dreary last days can be spent in grace.

What I recall of him: a thin and shadowy mustache and the gun. I remember the diminutive length of the barrel and its otherworldly gleam, backlit as it was by his flashlight. There was something drunken about the way he swayed, the unsteady manner in which he held his pistol, arm outstretched and wavering. I imagine he stumbled upon me after a few drinks with friends. "Hey, you there!" he called. "Stop! Police!" Picture this: a man in this light shouting, gun held unsteadily, as if by a puppeteer. I looked back toward him and said meekly, drawing on an innocence I could not have possessed, "Yes?"

"The hell are you doing?" he shouted from behind the blinding light.

I scoured my mind for explanations but found none. The truth sounded implausible; especially the truth. The silence was punctuated by the dog's pained cry. "This mutt bit my little brother," I said.

He kept the barrel trained on me, skeptical, but stepped closer. "Is he rabid?"

"I'm not sure, Officer."

Bent over the dog, he examined its dying body. Blood ran in thin streams through the grass, fanning out toward the edge of the street. It reminded me of the maps I studied in grade school, of the Amazon Basin with its web of crooked tributaries flowing to the sea.

"Where's your brother? Has he been seen by a doctor?"

I nodded. "He's with my mother at home," I said and waved my arm to indicate a place not far away in no particular direction. There was a glint of kindness in him, though I knew he didn't exactly believe me. I was not as accustomed to lying as you might think. I was afraid that he might see through me. So I continued. I told of my brother, the terrible bite, the awful scream I had heard, the red, fleshy face of the wound. His innocence, his shining eyes, his smile, his grace. I gave my brother all the qualities I lacked, made him beautiful and funny, as perfect as the blond puppets they use to sell soap on television. I was sweating, my heart racing, telling him of the jokes he told, the grades he got. A smart one, my brother! And then I gave him a name: "Manuel, but we call him Manolo, Manolito," I said, and the officer, gun in hand, softened.

"That's my name."

I looked up, not quite sure what he meant.

"I'm Manolo too," he said delicately, almost laughing. I chuckled nervously. The dog whimpered again. We faced each other in the still of the broad avenue and shared a smile.

The officer put his gun in the holster and moved to shake my hand. I wiped the blade of my knife on my thigh and put it down. We shook hands firmly, like men. "Manuel Carrión," he said.

And I said a name as well, though of course not mine and not Pintor.

He was a *cholo* like me, I knew it by the way he spoke. His father worked with his hands, as surely as he had cousins or brothers or friends who worked with their fists. He said he was pleased to meet me. "But what are you doing exactly? Killing this mutt?" he asked. "What will that accomplish?"

"I chased it down to see if it was rabid. The little bitch struggled with me. I guess I got carried away."

Carrión nodded and leaned over the dog once again. With his nightstick he poked it in its belly, eliciting a muted, pathetic yelp. He peered into its eyes for a particular shade of yellow and into its gaping mouth for the frothy telltale saliva. "No rabies. I think Manolito is going to be fine."

I was relieved for a brother I didn't have, for a bite that never was. My heart swelled. I imagined Manolito and his long, healthy days, running, playing among friends, his wound healed with not even a scar. I loved my fictitious brother.

Carrión was drunk and kind. If things had gone differently that black morning this episode might have become one of his favorite stories, when asked by a friend or cousin over a drink, "Hey, *cholo,* what's it like out there?" *Compa*, let me tell you about the night I helped a man kill a dog. No, that sounds too banal. *Hombre*, one time, I came upon a man decapitating a street mutt. . . . Who knows how he would tell the story now? Or if he would tell it at all?

"I used to be just like your Manolito," he was saying, "always getting into something. I liked to fight the big guys, but I was small. Always coming home with a broken this or a bruised that." Carrión spoke warmly now. "Are you taking him anywhere? The mutt, I mean."

"The doctor wanted to examine it," I said, "just to make sure."

Carrión nodded. "Of course. Good luck." He stood up to leave, unfolding himself, clearing grass from his knees. "You should put it out of its misery, you know. No point in being cruel."

I liked him. How simple and mundane.

I thanked the officer and assured him I would. We were pulling away, our good-byes restless on our tongues, when suddenly there was a noise, an abbreviated yelp. Looking up, I saw one of my *compañeros,* breathless, not thirty meters away, crouching savagely over a dog (white), holding it up by its muzzle, arm raised, knife in hand, poised to enter the fleshy underside of its neck. He had come down a side street and hadn't seen us until it was too late. Now he saw us and stopped. Confusion. Panic. Fearful, I reverted to form, abandoned my revolutionary training: I wanted to paint it, the brutal outline of a man at war with a mutt, caught in the act, frozen arms akimbo. I saw what I had looked like. Carrión looked my way, puzzled, then back at my *compañero,* and for a moment the three of us were caught in a triangle of wants, questions, and fears—a record skipping, a still life, a mutually-agreed-upon pause during which we each considered in silence the intricate and unfortunate relationships that connected us. An instant, nothing more.

Then Carrión drew his gun, just as I grasped my knife. My *compañero* let the dog drop unceremoniously to the sidewalk and took off running down the avenue away from the plaza. The white dog scampered off, still whimpering. And Carrión faced me, whatever shadow of friendship we had briefly cultivated lost in fog. My options ticked off before me like the outline of a brutal text: (A) stab the cop, quickly; (B) run, run fast, imbecile! (C) die like a man. And that was all my mind produced. Despairing, only my last choice made any sense. Can it even be called a choice? I held my blade, true, but weakly and without conviction. I made as if to rise, perhaps even run, but there was nothing there. And while I dawdled with limp and half-formed thoughts, Carrión acted: forgave me, inexplicably spared me, struck me with the butt of his gun and ran off in pursuit of my comrade—sealing his own fate.

He died that night.

Reeling, I fell toward what I recognized as death. It was only sleep. Into the grass, clutching my jaw, eyes closed, my sight swelled into black. Half-dead dogs howled and whimpered. In the distance, I heard a gunshot.

absence

On his second day in New York, Wari walked around Midtown looking halfheartedly for the airline office. He'd decided to forget everything. It was an early September day; the pleasant remains of summer made the city warm and inviting. He meandered in and out of sidewalk traffic, marveled at the hulking mass of the buildings, and confirmed, in his mind, that the city was the capital of the world. On the train, he'd seen break dancing and heard Andean flutes. He'd watched a Chinese man play a duet with Beethoven on a strange electronic harmonica. In Times Square, a Dominican man danced a frenetic merengue with a life-size doll. The crowds milled about, smiling, tossing money carelessly at the dancer, laughing when his hands slipped lustily over the curve of the doll's ass.

Wari didn't arrive at the airline office that day; he didn't smile at any nameless woman across the counter, or reluctantly pay the $100 fine to have his ticket changed. Instead he wandered, passed the time in intense meditation upon the exotic, upon the city, its odors and gleaming surfaces, and found himself in front of a group of workers digging a hole in the sidewalk at the base of a skyscraper. He sat down to have lunch and watch them. With metal-clawed machines they bored expertly though concrete. Wari had made a sandwich uptown that morning, and he ate distractedly now. The people passed in steady streams, bunching at corners and swarming across intersections the instant a light changed. From a truck, the men brought a thin sapling and lowered it into their newly dug hole. They filled it with dirt. Trees to fill holes, Wari thought, amused, but they weren't done. The workers smoked cigarettes and talked loudly among themselves and then one of them brought a wheelbarrow piled high with verdant grass cut into small squares. Sod. They laid the patches of leafy carpet out around the tree. Just like that. In the time it took Wari to eat, a hole was emptied and filled, a tree planted and adorned with fresh green grass. A wound created in the earth; a wound covered, healed, beautified. It was nothing. The city moved along, unimpressed, beneath a bright, late-summer sky.

He walked a little more and stopped in front of a group of Japanese artists drawing portraits for tourists. They advertised their skill with careful renderings of famous people, but Wari could only recognize a few. There was Bill Clinton and Woody Allen, and the rest were generically handsome in a way that reminded Wari of a hundred actors and actresses. It was the kind of work he could do easily. The artists' hands moved deftly across the parchment, shading here and there in swift strokes. Crowds slowed to watch, and the portraitists seemed genuinely oblivious, glancing up at their clients every now and then to make certain they weren't making any mistakes. When the work was done, the customer always smiled and seemed surprised at finding his own likeness on the page. Wari smiled too, found it folkloric, like everything he had seen so far in the city, worth remembering, somehow special in a way he couldn't yet name.

Wari had been invited to New York for an exhibit; serendipity, an entire chain of events born of a single conversation in a bar with an American tourist named Eric, a red-haired Ph.D. student in anthropology and committed do-gooder. He had acceptable Spanish and was a friend of a friend of Wari's who was still at the university. Eric and Wari had talked about Guayasamín and indigenous iconography, about cubism and the Paracas textile tradition of the Peruvian coast. They'd shared liter bottles of beer and laughed as their communication improved with each drink, ad-hoc Spanglish and pencil drawings on napkins. Eventually Eric made an appointment to see Wari's studio. He'd taken two paintings back to New York and set up an exhibit through his department. Everything culminated in an enthusiastic e-mail and an invitation on cream-colored bond paper. Wari had mulled it over for a few weeks, then spent most of his savings on a round-trip ticket. It was the only kind they sold. Once in New York and settled in, Wari buried the return ticket in the bottom of his bag, as if it were something radioactive. He didn't know what else to do with it. That first night, when the apartment had stilled, Wari dug into the suitcase and examined it. It had an unnatural density for a simple piece of paper. He dreamed that it glowed.

Wari found Leah, his host's girlfriend, making pasta. It was still light out, and Eric wasn't home yet. Wari wanted to explain exactly what he had seen and why it had impressed him, but he didn't have the words. She didn't speak Spanish but made up for it by smiling a lot and bringing him things. A cup of tea, a slice of toast. He accepted everything because he wasn't sure how to refuse. His English embarrassed him. While the water boiled, Leah stood at the edge of the living room. "Good day?" she said. "Did you have a good day?"

Wari nodded.

"Good," she said. She brought him the remote to the television, then turned into the small kitchen. Wari sat on the sofa and flipped through the channels, not wanting to be rude. He could hear Leah humming a song to herself. Her jeans were slung low on her hips. Wari made himself watch the television. Game shows, news programs, talk shows; trying to understand gave him a headache, and so he settled on a baseball game, which he watched with the volume down. The game was languid and hard to follow and, before long, Wari was asleep.

When he awoke, there was a plate of food in front of him. Leah was at the sink, washing her dish. Eric was home. *"Buenas noches!"* he called out grandly. "Good game?" He pointed at the television. Two players chatted on the mound, their faces cupped in their gloves.

"Yes," said Wari. He rubbed the sleep from his eyes.

Eric laughed. "The Yanks gonna get it back this year," he said. "They're the white team."

"I'm sorry," was all Wari could offer.

They spoke for a while in Spanish about the details of the exhibit, which was opening in two days. Wari's canvases stood against the wall, still wrapped in brown paper and marked FRAGILE. They would hang them tomorrow. "Did you want to work while you were here?" Eric asked. "I mean, paint? At my department, they said they could offer you a studio for a few weeks."

That had everything to do with the radioactive ticket interred at the bottom of his suitcase. Wari felt a tingling in his hands. He'd brought no brushes or paints or pencils or anything. He had no money for art supplies. He guessed it would be years before he would again. What would it be like *not* to paint?

"No, thank you," Wari said in English. He curled his fingers into a fist.

"Taking a vacation, huh? That's good. Good for you, man. Enjoy the city."

Wari asked about phone cards, and Eric said you could get them anywhere and cheap. Any bodega, corner store, pharmacy, newsstand. "We're connected," he said, and laughed. "Sell them right next to the Lotto tickets. You haven't called home?"

Wari shook his head. Did they miss him yet?

"You should." Eric settled into the couch. Leah had disappeared into the bedroom.

His host spoke to the flickering television while Wari ate.

The American embassy sits hunched against a barren mountain in a well-to-do suburb of Lima. It is an immense bunker with the tiled exterior of a fancy bathroom, its perimeter gate so far from the actual building that it would take a serious throw to hit even its lowest floor with a rock. A line gathers out front each morning before dawn, looping around the block, a hopeful procession of Peruvians with their sights on Miami or Los Angeles or New Jersey or anywhere. Since the previous September, after the attacks, the embassy had forced the line even farther out, beyond blue barricades, to the very edge of the wide sidewalk. Then there'd been a car bomb in March to welcome the visiting American president. Ten Peruvians had died, including a thirteen-year-old boy unlucky enough to be skateboarding near the embassy at exactly the wrong moment. His skull had been pierced by shrapnel. Now the avenue was closed to all but official traffic. The line was still there, every morning except Sundays, in the middle of the empty street.

Before his trip, Wari presented his letter and his fees and his paperwork. Statements of property, financials, university records, a list of exhibitions and gallery openings, certificates of birth and legal documents regarding a premature marriage and redemptive divorce. The entirety of his twenty-seven years, on paper. The centerpiece, of course, was Eric's invitation on letterhead from his university. Eric had let him know that this wasn't any old university. Wari gathered that he should say the name of the institution with reverence and all would know its reputation. Eric had assured him it would open doors.

Instead the woman said: We don't give ninety-day visas anymore.

Through the plastic window, Wari tried pointing at the invitation, at its gold letters and elegant watermark, but she wasn't interested. Come back in two weeks, she said.

He did. In his passport, Wari found a one-month tourist visa.

At the airport in Miami, Wari presented his paperwork once more, his passport and, separately, the invitation in its gilded envelope. To his surprise, the agent sent him straightaway to an interview room, without even glancing at the documents. Wari waited in the blank room, recalling how a friend had joked: "Remember to shave or they'll think you're Arab." Wari's friend had celebrated the remark by shattering a glass against the cement floor of the bar. Everyone had applauded. Wari could feel the sweat gathering in the pores on his face. He wondered how bad he looked, how tired and disheveled. How dangerous. The stale, recycled air from the plane compartment was heavy in his lungs. He could feel his skin darkening beneath the fluorescent lights.

An agent came in, shooting questions in English. Wari did his best. "An artist, eh?" the agent said, examining the paperwork.

Wari folded his fingers around an imaginary brush and painted circles in the air.

The agent waved Wari's gesture away. He looked through the papers, his eyes settling finally on the bank statement. He frowned.

"You're going to New York?" he asked. "For a month?"

"In Lima, they give to me one month," Wari said carefully.

The agent shook his head. "You don't have the money for that kind of stay." He looked at the invitation and then pointed to the paltry figure at the bottom of the bank statement. He showed it to Wari, who muffled a nervous laugh. "Two weeks. And don't get any ideas," the agent said. "That's generous. Get your ticket changed when you get to New York."

He stamped Wari's burgundy passport with a new visa and sent him on his way.

At baggage claim, Wari found his paintings in a stack next to an empty carousel. He made his way through customs, answering more questions before being let through. He waited patiently while they searched his suitcase, rifling through his clothes. His paintings were inspected with great care, and here the golden letter finally served a purpose. Customs let him through. Wari felt dizzy, the shuffling noise of the airport suddenly narcotic, sleep calling him to its protective embrace. Ninety days is a humane length of time, he thought. Enough time to come to a decision and find its cracks. To look for work and organize contingencies. To begin imagining the permanence of good-byes. It wasn't as if Wari had nothing to lose. He had parents, a brother, good friends, a career just beginning in Lima, an ex-wife. If he left it behind? Even a month spent in meditation—ambling about a new city, working out the kinks of a foreign language—might be space enough to decide. But two weeks? Wari thought it cruel. He counted days on his fingers: twenty-four hours after his paintings came down, he would be illegal. Wari had imagined that the right decision would appear obvious to him, if not right away, then certainly before three months had passed. But there was no chance of clarity in fourteen days. Wari walked through the Miami airport as if he'd been punched in the face. His feet dragged. He made his flight to La Guardia just as the doors were closing, and was stopped again at the jetway, his shoes examined by a plastic-gloved woman who refused to return his weak smiles. On the plane, Wari slept with his face flush against the oval window. There was nothing to see anyway. It was an overcast day in South Florida, no horizon, no turquoise skies worthy of postcards, nothing except the gray expanse of a wing and its contrails, blooming at the end like slivers of smoke.

Leah woke him with apologies. "I have to work," she said softly. "You couldn't have slept through it anyway." She smiled. Her hair was pulled back in a ponytail. She smelled clean. Leah made jewelry, and his bedroom, which was actually the living room, was also her workshop.

"Is okay," Wari said, sitting up on the couch, taking care to hide his morning erection.

Leah grinned as Wari fumbled awkwardly with the sheet. "I've seen plenty of that, trust me," she said. "I wake up with Eric every morning."

Wari felt his face turn red. "Is lucky," he said.

She laughed.

"Where is? Eric?" he asked, cringing at his pronunciation.

"Studying. Work. He teaches undergrads. *Young students*," she said, translating young, in gestures, as small.

Wari pictured Eric, with his wide, pale face and red hair, teaching miniature people, tiny humans who looked up to him for knowledge. He liked that Leah had tried. He understood much more than he could say, but how could she know that?

He watched her for a while, filing metal and twisting bands of silver into circles. He liked the precision of her work, and she didn't seem to mind him. Leah burnished a piece, filed and sanded, bent metal with tools that seemed too brusque for her delicate hands. She held a hammer with authority, she was a woman with purpose. It was a powerful display. "I'm finishing up," she said finally, "and then you can come with me. I know a Peruvian you can talk to."

He showered and ate a bowl of cold cereal before they left for downtown. The Peruvian she knew was named Fredy. She didn't know where he was from exactly, though she was sure he'd told her. Fredy worked a street fair on Canal. Leah had won him over with a smile a few years before, and now he let her sell her jewelry on consignment. Every couple of weeks, she went down with new stuff, listened as Fredy catalogued what had sold and what hadn't, and to his opinionated take on why. He lived in New Jersey now, Leah said, and had married a Chinese woman. "They speak to each other in broken English. Isn't that amazing?"

Wari agreed.

"It must say something about the nature of love, don't you think?" Leah asked. "They have to trust each other so completely. That window of each other that they know in English is so small compared to everything they are in their own language."

Wari wondered. The train rattled on its way downtown. But

it's always like that, he wanted to say, you can never know anyone completely. Instead he was silent.

"Do you understand me when I speak?" Leah asked. "If I speak slowly?"

"Of course," Wari said, and he did, but felt helpless to say much more. He noted the descending numbered streets at every stop, and followed their subterranean progress on the map. A sticker covered the southern end of the island. They got off before they reached that veiled area. On Canal, only a few blocks was enough to remind Wari of Lima: that density, that noise, that circus. The air was swollen with foreign tongues. He felt comfortable in a way, but didn't mind at all when Leah took his arm and led him swiftly through the crowds of people. He bumped shoulders with the city, like walking against a driving rain.

Fredy turned out to be Ecuadorian, and Leah couldn't hide her embarrassment. She turned a rose color that reminded Wari of the dying light at dusk. Wari and Fredy both reassured her it was nothing.

"We're brother countries," Fredy said.

"We share border and history," said Wari.

The Ecuadorian was all obsequious smiles, spoke of the peace treaty that was signed only a few years before. Wari played along, shook Fredy's hand vigorously until Leah seemed at ease with her mistake. Then she and Fredy talked business, haggling in a teasing way that seemed more like flirting, and of course Leah won. When this was finished, she excused herself, and drifted away to the other stands, leaving Wari and Fredy alone.

When she was out of earshot, Fredy turned to Wari. "Don't ask me for work, *compadre*," he said, frowning. "It's hard enough for me."

Wari was taken aback. "Who asked you for work? I've got work, *cholo*."

"Sure you do."

Wari ignored him, inspected the table laid out with small olive forks bent into ridiculous earrings. At the other end, there were black-and-white photos of Andean peaks, silvery and snowcapped, and others of ruined fortresses of stone and colonial churches. The scenes were devoid of people: landscapes or buildings or scattered rocks carved by Incas, unified by their uninhabited emptiness. "There's no people," Wari said.

"They emigrated," sneered Fredy.

"This shit sells?"

"Good enough."

"That's my girl, you know," Wari said all of a sudden, and he liked the tone of the lie, the snap of it, and the way the Ecuadorian looked up, surprised.

"The gringa?"

"Yeah."

"I bet she is," said Fredy.

Then two customers appeared, a young woman with her boyfriend. Fredy switched to English, heavily accented but quite acceptable, and pointed to various objects, suggesting earrings that matched the woman's skin tone. She tried on a pair, Fredy dutifully held the mirror up for her, her distracted boyfriend checking out the photos. Wari wondered where Leah had gone off to. The woman turned to him. "What do you think?" she asked, looking back and forth between Wari and Fredy.

"Is very nice," Wari said.

"Like a million bucks," said Fredy.

"Where's this from?" she asked, fingering the lapis lazuli stone.

"Peru," said Wari.

Fredy shot him a frown. "From the Andes," he said.

"Trev," she called to her boyfriend. "It's from Peru! Isn't it nice?"

She pulled out a twenty and Fredy made change. He wrapped the earrings in tissue paper and handed her a card. The couple walked away, chatting. Wari and Fredy didn't speak.

Leah reappeared and Wari made sure to touch her, thoughtlessly, as if it meant nothing at all. He could feel Fredy watching them, studying each of their movements. "Did you tell Fredy about your opening?" she asked Wari.

He shook his head. "So modest," Leah said and filled in the details and, to his delight, exaggerated its importance and weight. Wari felt like a visiting dignitary, someone famous.

Wari put his arm around Leah. She didn't stop him. Fredy said it would be difficult to make it.

"Okay, but maybe?" she asked.

"Please come," added Wari, not worrying about his pronunciation.

Leaving is no problem. It's exciting actually; in fact, it's drug. It's the staying gone that will kill you. This is the handed-down wisdom of the immigrant. You hear it from the people who wander home, after a decade away. You hear about the euphoria that passes quickly; the new things that lose their newness and, soon after, their capacity to amuse you. Language is bewildering. You tire of exploring. Then the list of things you miss multiplies beyond all reason, nostalgia clouding everything: in memory, your country is clean and uncorrupt, the streets are safe, the people universally warm, and the food consistently delicious. The sacred details of your former life appear and reappear in strange iterations, in a hundred waking dreams. Your pockets fill with money, but your heart feels sick and empty.

Wari was prepared for all this.

In Lima, he rounded up a few friends and said his good-byes. Tentative, equivocal good-byes. Good-byes over drinks, presented as jokes, gentle laughter before the *poof* and the vanishing—that Third World magic. I may be back, he told everyone, or I may not. He moved two boxes of assorted possessions into the back room of his parents' house. He took a few posters off the walls, covered the little holes with Wite-Out. He encouraged his mother to rent out his room for extra money if he didn't come home in a month. She cried, but just a little. His brother wished him luck. Wari offered a toast to family at Sunday dinner and promised to come home one day soon. He embraced his father and accepted the crisp $100 bill the old man slipped into his hand. And in the last days before leaving, Wari and Eric exchanged feverish e-mails, ironing out the fine points of the exhibit: the exact size of the canvases, the translated bio, the press release. All the formalities of a real opening, but for Wari, it was so much noise and chatter. The only solid things for him were the ticket and the runway and the plane and the obligatory window seat for a last, fading view of Lima. The desert purgatory, the approaching northern lights.

I'm ready, he thought.

And if no one questioned him, it's because the logic was self-evident. What would he do there? How long could he live at home? A divorced painter, sometime teacher—what does an artist do in a place like that? In America, you can sweep floors and make money, if you're willing to work—you are willing to work, aren't you, Wari?

Yes, I am.

At anything? Outdoor work? Lifting, carting, cleaning?

Anything.

And that was it. What other questions were there? He'd be fine.

Only his mother gave voice to any concerns. "Is it about Elie?" she asked a few days before he traveled. Wari had been expecting this question. Elie, his ex-wife, whom he loved and whom he hated. At least there were no children to grow up hating him. Wari was relieved it was over, believed she must be as well.

"No, Ma," he said. "It has nothing to do with her."

So his mother smiled and smiled and smiled.

In Eric's apartment, Wari daydreamed. He dressed up the lie about Leah. He lay on the couch, composing e-mails about her to his friends back home, describing the shape of her body, the colors of her skin. The solution to his fourteen-day quandary: marry her and stay, marry her and go. Marry her and it would be all the same. He imagined falling in love in monosyllables, in nods and smiles and meaningful gestures. Telling Leah the story of his life in pictograms: His modest family home. The drab, charcoal colors of his native city. His once-happy marriage and its dissolving foundations, crumbling from the inside into a perfect parody of love. It was early afternoon and Leah readied herself for a waitressing job. The shower ran. Through the thin walls he could hear the sound of the water against her body. Her light brown hair went dark when it was wet. He closed his eyes and pictured her naked body. Then Elie's. Wari turned on the television, let its noise fill the living room. Almost a year from the attacks, and the inevitable replays had begun. He changed the channel, his mind wandered: Fredy on a train home to his Chinese wife, wondering if what Wari had boasted of was true. Elie, somewhere in Lima, not even aware he was gone. Leah, in the shower, not thinking of him. On every channel, buildings collapsed in clouds of dust, and Wari watched on mute, listening hopefully to Leah's water music.

Wari rapped twice on the wooden door. This was years ago. "*Chola,*" he called to the woman who would be his wife. "*Chola*, are you there?"

But Elie wasn't there. She'd left the music on loud to discourage burglars. She lived in Magdalena, a crumbling district by the sea, in a neighborhood of stereos playing loudly in empty apartments. Fourteen-year-old kids cupped joints in their palms and kept a lookout for cops. They played soccer in the streets and tossed pebbles at the moto-taxis. Wari knocked again. "She ain't home," someone called from the street. Wari knew she wasn't, but he wanted to see her. He wanted to kiss her and hold her and tell her his good news.

He was a younger, happier version of himself.

My good news, baby: his first exhibit in a gallery in Miraflores. A real opening with wine, a catalogue, and they'd promised him press, maybe even half a column interview in one of the Sunday magazines. This is what he wanted to tell her.

Wari knocked some more. He hummed along to the melody that played in her apartment. He pulled pen and paper from his bag and composed a note for her, in English. They were both studying it at an institute, Elie with much less enthusiasm. English is tacky, she'd say. She mourned the passing of Spanish, the faddish use of gringo talk. It was everywhere: on television, in print, on the radio. In cafés, their peers spoke like this: *"Sí, pero asi es la gente nice. No tienen ese* feeling." Why are you learning that language, *acomplejado,* my dear Wari, you just paint and you'll be fine. She made him laugh and that was why he loved her. On a piece of paper torn from a notebook, he wrote:

I come see you, but instead meet your absence.

It's perfect, he thought. He put a *W* in the corner, just because—as if anyone else would come to her home and leave a note like this. He tacked it to the door and walked down to the street, music serenading the walls of empty apartments. Music that slipped out into the street. He had nothing to do but wait for her. A kid on the corner scowled at him, but Wari smiled back. It was late afternoon, the last dying light of day.

The show went up, but the reception was sparsely attended. "It's a bad time," said Eric, with Leah on his arm. "The anniversary has everyone on edge."

"On edge," Wari asked, "is like scared?"

"Just like that," Leah said.

Wari didn't care. He was scared too. And not because the world could explode, or because Manhattan could sink into the sea. Real fears. His paintings were glowing beneath the bright lights. A handful of people filtered in and out, sipping champagne from plastic cups. Already there was something foreign about his paintings, as if they were the work of someone else, a man he used to know, an acquaintance from a distant episode in his life. There was nothing special about them, he decided. They exist, as I exist, and that is all.

The grandiose illusion of the exile is that they are all back home, your enemies and your friends, voyeurs all, watching you. Everything has gained importance because you are away. Back home, your routines were only that. Here, they are portentous, significant. They have the weight of discovery. Can they see me? In this city, this cathedral? In this New York gallery? Never mind that it was nearly empty, and a hundred blocks from the neighborhoods where art was sold. Not for himself, but for their benefit, Wari would manufacture the appropriate amount of excitement. Make them all happy. I'm doing it, Ma, he'd say over the static. It's a bad connection, but I know now everything will be all right.

Afterward, Eric and Leah took Wari out for drinks with some friends. He could tell they felt bad, as if they had let him down. Eric complained about student apathy. Lack of engagement, he called it. His department was in disarray, he said, they hadn't done a very good job of advertising. Leah nodded in solemn agreement. It was all words. Nothing Wari said could convince his host that he really didn't care. *I used you,* he wanted to say. *I'm not a painter anymore.* But that seemed so cruel, so ungrateful, and still untrue.

"Is no problem," he repeated over and over. "We have good time."

"Yes, yes, but still . . . I feel *bad*."

Americans always feel bad. They wander the globe carrying this opulent burden. They take digital photographs and buy folk art, feeling a dull disappointment in themselves, and in the world. They bulldoze forests with tears in their eyes. Wari smiled. He wanted to say he understood, that none of it was Eric's fault. It's what had to happen. He took Eric's hand. "Thank you," Wari said, and squeezed.

The bar was warm and lively. The televisions broadcasted baseball games from a dozen cities. Eric's friends congratulated Wari, clapped him on the back. *"Muy bien!"* they shouted gregariously. They wouldn't let him spend a single dollar. They bought round after round until the lights from the beer signs were blurred neon arabesques. Wari felt it nearly impossible to understand a single word of their shouted conversations. There was a girl, a woman who kept making eyes at him. She was slight and had a fragile goodness to her. Wari watched her whisper with Leah, and they looked his way and smiled. He smiled back.

"I liked your paintings very much," she said later. The night was winding down. Already a few people had left. Leah and Eric had separated from the group. They kissed each other and laughed and, by the way they looked into each other's eyes, Wari could tell they were in love. It made him feel silly.

He was ignoring the woman in front of him. "Thank you," he said.

"They're so violent."

"I do not intend that."

"It's what I saw."

"Is good you see this. Violence sometime happen."

"I'm Ellen," she said.

"Is nice name. My ex-wife name Elie."

"You're Wari."

"I am."

"How long will you stay?"

"I have ten more days on the visa," Wari said.

"Oh."

"But I do not know."

There were more drinks and more intimate shouting over the cacophony of the bar. Ellen had a sweet smile and lips he could see himself kissing. His hand had fallen effortlessly on her knee. In the corner of the bar, Leah and Eric kissed again and again. *How long will you stay I do not know. Howlongwilly-oustayIdonotknow.* Wari wanted to drop his glass on the floor, but he was afraid it wouldn't shatter. He was afraid no one would applaud, no one would understand the beauty of that sound. The days were vanishing. Then he was in the street and Ellen was teaching him how to hail a cab. You have to be aggressive, she said. Does she think we don't have cabs? he wondered, shocked. Does she think we ride mules? Just as quickly, he didn't care. She meant nothing by it. He could feel the planet expanding, its details effaced. Who is this woman? What city is this? The evening was warm, and the sky, if you looked straight up, was a deep indigo. They were downtown. His head was swimming in drink. I should call my mother, he thought, and tell her I'm alive. I should call Elie and tell her I'm dead.

They stood on the street corner. Cab after yellow cab rolled past Wari's outstretched arm. He was no good at it. Wari turned to find Ellen in a daze, gazing down the avenue.

"They were there, you know. Just right there," Ellen said. She reached for his hand.

They were quiet. She pointed with two fingers in the direction of the southern horizon, toward the near end of the island. Wari stared at the yawning space in the sky, a wide and hollow nothing.

the visitor

It had been three months and I thought things would have gotten easier. The children still cried at night. They still asked about their mother. On clear mornings, I took them to the cemetery, which was all that was left of the old town. From that hill we could see the remains of the valley, and the sharp scar where the mountain had slipped. The planes flew only on clear, cloudless days, and we watched for them in the skies above us: whirling, seesawing, their shaky wings trembling in the mountain wind. The children waved. We counted the parachutes drifting down and down. It was a game we played. I taught Mariela and Ximena to differentiate between German and French as we sifted through the aid packages. I helped Efraín pull the parachutes from the mud and clean them off.

The first day we huddled together to stay warm. The sky was heavy with dust after the landslide. We'd been at the cemetery burying the little one, who was only a few days old when he died, who Erlinda, my wife, hadn't had the heart to name. The children didn't understand. Erlinda had stayed in town, still recovering. We lowered him into the earth. Then there was a shaking. The mountain broke free. I held our three children close to me. A stew of ice and rock and mud rumbled down the valley.

We stayed at the cemetery that first night. Some of the coffins had been shaken from the earth. I made a lean-to with the planks of wood. The earth shook every hour or so, and I was afraid. Only the summit of the cemetery hill was still poking out from beneath the slippery mud. There was just room enough for me and my children.

On the second day, the sun came out, and the mud began to dry. I took two of the longest planks and told the children to wait for me. Efraín wanted to come, but I told him to stay and take care of his sisters. Help is coming, I said. I laid the planks out one in front of the other, and made my way across the mud toward where our house had been. I oriented myself by the plaza, which I could still make out. The tops of the four palm trees rose out of the mud, but the cathedral and the other buildings had been buried. I saw no one. The planks sunk a little into the mud as I walked.

I stepped over the buried town. We'd moved here from the south end of the valley when it was time to start a family. We'd made a life here. I tended herds I did not own. Erlinda sold what she could in the market. We worked and we saved. We'd tried to buy a small plot of land on the eastern folds of the mountains, but had been spurned. Those lands are reserved for important families, they'd told us, not for you. Just before the youngest was buried, we'd talked of leaving. To the city, to the sea. I remember Erlinda and her confusion. We worried about our children, about the future. We would never leave. This was home. It had been home.

I made it, finally, to where my house had stood, to where my wife must have been buried. I'd taken a cross from the cemetery, scavenged from one of the wrecked graves, and I planted it in the mud above my home. Erlinda, I prayed, had felt no pain and hadn't had time to be afraid. She had died in her sleep, I prayed.

Across the valley, the mountain sides were green and blooming. My children were hungry. I sat and prayed, and then took my planks and continued on toward the hills.

I found herbs and fruits there, and grazing sheep and goats that now had no owner other than me. The sun warmed my cheeks. Across the valley, across the muddy strip of earth, I saw the cemetery hill. The children sat together; I waved to them. We would be better off here, I decided. These were the best lands. I went back for the children. While the girls waited, Efraín and I made two more trips, crossing the thick mud with careful steps, carrying more planks. With the remains of the shattered coffins, we made a new home on the eastern slopes.

In the weeks after, Efraín seemed to be growing every day, and I was proud. He took care of the girls. He made my life easier. The girls asked him about their mother because they knew not to ask me anymore. Efraín gave them the same simple answer I had given them: that things were different now. This would usually set them crying, Mariela folding herself into her sister's embrace. I would hold them, but I had nothing to give them. I tried to be strong. I dreamed of Erlinda every night. Each day I went to see her, to tell her about the children, about our new home. I told her I missed her. Every week or so, I pulled the cross out and replanted it so it wouldn't tilt or lean as the mud settled. From our new home we could see everything, and everything, I told Erlinda, was ours: the cemetery hill, the four palm trees, the green eastern slopes, and the grazing herds. Erlinda, my wife, was resting.

Some days I stole away from the children. Efraín disappeared with his sisters to play and I to gather parachutes from the hillsides. I would find myself crying. I cried for the town and for my wife, for myself and the children. I cried for my fourth child, the buried child. The children seemed to have forgotten him: his smallness, his labored breathing, and even the events of that day. And I tried to forget him too: in the way of our grandparents, who withheld their love from a child until he had survived two winters. When I was Efraín's age, I lost a sister. For a time, our home was quiet and heavy, but then she was buried and never spoken of again.

The children survived my moods. Sometimes I asked, "Do you remember where we used to live?" and their blank stares told me they hadn't understood my question. I envied them and their youthful amnesia. Under the sweep of mountain sky, I felt alone.

"Where did we live?" I asked them.

"With Mother," was all they ever said. We gave our emptiness a name. That name was Erlinda.

So we stayed there, on the other side of the valley from the cemetery, on the foothills above the martyred town. Parachutes slipped through the heavy clouds, swinging gently in the passing wind. No one came to see the town or its graves. We waited. We were there when the visitor came.

His name was Alejo. He carried a bundle of clothes wrapped in a blanket. He'd come from over the mountains, from the city. "I've been walking," he told me, "for two weeks." Alejo yawned as he sat, and I heard his bones creaking. "I have news."

"Tell it then," I said.

"There are twenty thousand dead in the city."

"Twenty thousand?" I asked.

The visitor nodded. He took off his shoes.

"And in the north?"

"Seven thousand when I left."

"The south?"

"At last count, sixteen thousand."

My head felt light. "On the coast?" I asked, though I knew no one on the coast.

"There are no towns left standing."

"My God," I said.

His face was cracked by the wind. He rubbed his feet. Ximena brought us tea in earthen bowls. We sat quietly.

"What are people saying?" I asked.

He cupped his bowl in his calloused hands. He let the steam kiss his face. "They're hardly speaking at all."

It was getting cold.

From the pile of clothes, Mariela brought our visitor a jacket. "Guess where this jacket came from!" she asked cheerfully. "Guess!"

The visitor smiled gently and shrugged his shoulders. We were all bundled and wearing the bright clothing of survivors.

"France!" my daughter said, beaming.

I smiled. "We counted thirteen parachute drops in one day," I said.

"Thirteen?"

My son and I had collected nearly fifty parachutes. We would build tents with them, for when the rains come.

We sat in silence for a moment.

"What do we have for our visitor?" I called to the children. We'd been inundated with aid, some of it useful, some of it less so. A box of oversize bathing suits from Holland. Postcards from New York that wished us well. A package of neckties from

Denmark. I'd picked a red one, which I used to tie back my hair. Efraín offered Alejo a selection of ties. Erlinda would have been proud. "Please take one," he said, bowing ceremoniously.

The visitor picked an orange tie and smiled at me. He wore it as a headband, then picked a shorter green one, which he tied on Efraín. "We're a tribe now," the visitor said, laughing. Efraín smiled too.

It was overcast, the sky a color of bone. The fog sank from the silver mountains. "How many did you lose here, friend?" the visitor asked.

We could still see the cross. I pointed across the muddy plain at my resting wife. "Only one," I said.

Efraín had picked out headbands for his sisters. My children were a row of Danish neckties. "Only one," they said in a chorus.

war by candlelight

I. Oxapampa, 1989

The day before a stray bomb buried him in the Peruvian jungle, Fernando sat with José Carlos and together they meditated on death.

They were childhood friends. Three decades before, you might have found them together on the steps of the cathedral, sharing a piece of bread, tossing pebbles at the stray dogs that came to lick the crumbs at their feet. Or on hands and knees, playing marbles in the dusty courtyard of José Carlos's house on Tarapacá. Such trivial things come to mind now, Fernando thought. A lifetime's supply of meaningless memories. He could make out the dark blue tint of the sky above. Later it would rain.

They sat at the edge of the campsite. Here, hidden in a tangle of vines and leaves and wrapped in a tarp, were the explosives. Fernando and José Carlos had slipped away from the others, had chosen this place to talk. They shared a rolled cigarette and a stale piece of bread, and agreed both were the worst they'd ever tasted. The bread especially. "Tougher than flesh," José Carlos said. "Worse than prison food."

"Worse than your mother's cooking," Fernando added. He watched for a smile spreading across his friend's face.

But José Carlos looked worn, unshaven, and grim, wearing a frayed white shirt and a straw hat that unraveled at its edges. His eyes drifted, unfocused, and his hands, crisscrossed with nicks and scratches, twitched almost imperceptibly. Fernando watched him closely, looking for answers in José Carlos's face, wondering how they had come to this place and why. Though he had tried to forget, it was no use: the heat was murder, the air unbreathable. A kind of paralysis gripped Fernando those last days. He found himself unable to concentrate on the present. Instead his brain was clogged with memories half-eaten by moths and flies, incomplete records of moments in no semblance of order: Arequipa at night, circa 1960, in the middle of the lonely street looking up, all sky and silence; the women who had cared for him, from birth through childhood and beyond; his wife, Maruja, his daughter, Carmen, fragile, beautiful, and above all, his.

It couldn't help to think too much of those he left behind. Each of the previous four mornings Fernando had woken to the prickling tiptoes of insects meandering among legs or arms. Each day, as the jungle closed in on them, they took to the machetes for a half hour in the late afternoon, hacking and swinging and beating it back. The jungle was their greatest enemy. Unattended food vanished in minutes, with living things bursting from the soil to retrieve it, digest it, destroy it. It was not life that he thought of in the jungle, beneath the forest's thick canopy, in the darkness.

"Does this place have a name?" José Carlos wondered aloud. "Have the mapmakers made it here yet?"

Of course they had not. Oxapampa had a name, but it was a

three-day hike from here, and along the way they had passed nothing but forest and rising heat.

It was Fernando who suggested they name it. But what kind of name did this patch of earth deserve? Indigenous? Revolutionary? Should they call it Tarapacá, in honor of their old street?

They settled on Paris, where poets lived, and ate their bread in silence.

In the life he had left behind José Carlos was a professor of philosophy, a life he would survive to reclaim. Fernando could see him trying to laugh but unable. "I'm not scared that they'll catch me," José Carlos said. "I'm not afraid to die."

"To die in Paris!" Fernando said.

José Carlos frowned. "I'm not joking, Negro."

Fernando, his clothes soaked with sweat, felt his body melting into the infinite jungle. José Carlos was right: the time for jokes had passed. These conversations about death made him tired. It was all anyone ever spoke of. What point could there be in it? This moment was all they had worked for in the last fifteen years. The country was at war. The crisis they had foreseen in their youth had finally arrived. It was too late to give up, too late to change course. They were less than three weeks from the New Year and a new decade. Fernando was forty-one years old. His daughter, Carmen, whom he would never see again, was two and a half.

"Me neither," he said. "I'm not afraid to die."

II. War by Candlelight, 1983

They had a plan if they ever came under fire: "scatter."

Not sophisticated or elegant, but real.

This is a coward's war, Fernando thought, when at the first sign of trouble, I am told to run breathlessly into the heart of the jungle, without stopping or looking back.

"You're no good to us dead, Fernando. We have enough martyrs."

There was too much talk of comradeship and brotherhood for those instructions to sit well. He did his work, hoping it would never come to that. But he was touring the camps in the North, in San Martín, when shots were fired. There was no time to think. An army battalion had stumbled upon them in the steep, forested hills. No tactics or strategies involved, only the logic of a war fought blindly in the darkness of the jungle: a scared soldier fires a shot; a frightened rebel shoots back. Both are too young to do little else but bury their doubts in violence, and suddenly everyone is running and the forest is aflame.

Everything he had been taught came to him with the clarity of intuition: "We must only engage the enemy on our terms."

Neither side sees the other.

"Scatter."

In the jungle the trees have fingers and hands, the vines trip you up. You run because death is chasing, because the only way to escape is alone. Fernando fought through the jungle for two days before finding his way to the narrow path along the ridge where they were to regroup. Two days, alone, following trickles of water and minute hints of shadow, calling him first this way, then that. His instincts were urban, made for estimating bus routes and arrival times, not for looking to the skies for clues. He found his way, but not before wondering aloud if this were the place and the moment God had chosen for him to die. He met up with his comrades, they counted heads, quietly mourned the missing without abandoning hope that they might step out of the jungle, shaken but breathing. What had happened? No one knew anything more than he did. They licked their wounds and gathered their resolve. Back into the trees, to wander, to engage the enemy, to fight the people's war.

But Fernando's tour ended there. In five weeks, he had never carried a gun. He had never laid an explosive. The war, he thought—his war—had amounted to walking circles through the forest, going hungry, and picking insects off his skin each morning. Trying to stay dry. Praying not to be found.

He boarded a bus in a provincial town and began his journey back to the coast. He wondered if people knew, if he would ever feel completely safe again. Three times the bus was emptied while soldiers searched the baggage hold for weapons. His forged identification papers were inspected by police at isolated mountain checkpoints. Each time Fernando tensed, but they let him through. "Go on," the soldiers said, and Fernando did his best not to act surprised, or worse, grateful. The ride home took two days. Fernando ate in minuscule mountain towns, on wooden benches that sagged beneath the weight of a half dozen bleary-eyed passengers. He did his best to sleep, his head bumping against the fogged-over window. He returned to Lima overjoyed to be alive. It was a relief so overwhelming it made him dizzy.

That first night back he told Maruja he wouldn't leave Lima again. She'd thrown her arms around him when he first came in but had almost immediately pulled away. She avoided him, wouldn't even look at him. "What's wrong?" he asked.

There were lines on her face he'd never noticed before. She bit her lip. Her eyes were red. "I thought you were dead," Maruja said.

Their apartment was cramped and small. He sat at the

kitchen table while she prepared the candles and the matches. They listened for the rumble of war's progress, for a bomb to scratch out the quiet, the calm. It happened almost every night now. Electrical towers felled by explosives, a hammer and sickle ignited on the hillsides. It was best to be prepared. A pot of water boiled on the stove. He skimmed six weeks' worth of newspapers. She'd saved him the front pages, thrown away the rest. She summarized for him: "While you were dead," Maruja told him, "things got worse."

She wasn't going to forgive him easily. From the stack of scattered pages, she pulled one. It was dated from a week and a half before, and told of the ambush he'd fled. There were photos of the camp, of the weapons seized, and one of six lifeless bodies laid in a neat row. Though their faces were covered, Fernando knew them. They were his men, his friends. They had names. He recognized them by the shoes they wore.

An hour later, they heard it: *boom.*

Lights flickered and faded.

In the tense dark of their apartment, it occurred to him that he wanted a child. It struck him as exactly right. He felt embarrassed to tell Maruja. He said nothing. His entire body ached. They listened in darkness to the radio announcer calmly describing the evening's events. The room glowed orange.

Sometime in the middle of the night, when she was asleep and the candle had gone out, he reached for her.

It took him weeks to regain his courage. The city appeared strange to him, and his two-day walk through the jungle still had the glow of an apparition. Some mornings he woke and caught himself dreaming of insects and flittering birds. Bombs. Running. He caught himself paying attention to strangers' shoes. Every day he thought of the child he wanted. He rode through the city, debating quietly with himself: a child was a preposterous thing to want at a time like this. Absurd. Dangerous. Around him, men and women were disappearing, people dying. It was no time to indulge in bourgeois fantasies. But he let himself imagine fatherhood and a hundred other conventional pleasures: a small house with a courtyard, an olive tree, and a tomato plant, a childhood like the one he'd had. Sometimes Fernando imagined himself as an old man, the war long since over and nearly forgotten. His children now grown, his grandchildren asking to be told stories. What stories would he and Maruja tell them? Stories of survival, perhaps: How we fled Lima, Fernando mused. How we escaped the war.

He was riding a bus one day when a young woman got on. Visibly pregnant, her belly pushed dramatically against her dress. She was pretty, her lustrous hair in a single braid, woven as thick as rope. He gave her his seat. She didn't thank him, or notice him hovering over her. The bus stumbled on, filled past capacity. Fernando kept his right hand in his pocket, holding his wallet, and the other he placed on the back of the pregnant woman's seat. What was he expecting? He wanted her to pull out a book of baby names, or a spool of yarn to knit tiny socks. She didn't. She chewed gum. There was nothing at all special about her except that beautiful roundness. Fernando couldn't help but stare. He tensed. Finally, she opened her bag, pulled out a newspaper, and turned it to the crossword. Then there was a pushing and a jostling on the bus, and someone was being robbed at that exact moment. Everyone knew it: a dozen pairs of eyes darting back and forth, accusing. The pregnant woman sat still, unconcerned, nibbling on the tip of her plastic pen. By the time he got off, she'd fallen asleep with the crossword half-done in her lap.

That night, like every night, he and Maruja sat by candlelight, listening to the radio. But he had heard enough: the news was uniformly dismal, and it did no good to hear it all. He turned it off. He told her: "Let's have a baby."

They sat close together and spoke in circles about the child, he saying yes, she saying no.

He'd already heard her arguments, of course. They were his own. He suspected they were true, but as she voiced them, they sounded profoundly pessimistic. Hadn't they always believed in a future? Had they come to this place so soon: were they this defeated already? He held his head in his hands and cried, Maruja stroking his hair, wrapping the black curls around her fingers. Did she have to hurt him like this? She took his glasses and laid them on the nightstand. Their bed, resting on cinder blocks, creaked as she stretched. With the flame clinging to the wick, orange light gliding along the walls, Fernando told her for the first time of the jungle. "I walked for days. Alone. I could barely see the sky, and I was sure someone was following me."

Maruja touched him, kissed him. She laid him down and undressed him. Fernando could scarcely keep his eyes open. It wasn't such a terrible thing to want, was it? The city was full of children.

"We can't, Nano." She sighed deeply. "I can't."

Maruja had two boys from her first marriage, the oldest now nearing fifteen. Fernando was good with her children. He took them to San Miguel or to the movies. The noise and chaos of parenting seemed to excite him, to energize him, and Fernando would drive the children, singing and shouting. When they played soccer, Fernando would feed the pass that let his stepchildren shine. They were the youngest players on the field, but he made them feel welcome, wanted. He picked them first. Maruja's children were in love with Fernando. They let him know. All of this, Fernando thought, was proof. Hasn't she seen me with them? "I'd be a good father," he said.

"For how long?" she asked.

III. Drive, 1987

The call came before dawn, a phone ringing, startling him from dreams. He hoped it wouldn't wake the baby. Maruja didn't stir. It was a man's voice. He seemed to know who Fernando was. "Can you drive?" the voice asked.

Fernando dressed without turning on the lights. The station wagon started on the second try. He drove along deserted city streets, avoiding the known roadblocks, hoping not to stumble upon others. They changed every night. He had documents ready—real ones—and an excuse, a story to tell, if it came to that: "I'm going to pick up my brother. He's a doctor. My little girl is sick."

It was four-thirty in the morning. He idled his car on the fourth block of Avenida Bolivia and waited. He blew hot air on his hands. His neck hurt, his mouth was dry. It was cold, but in an hour, the darkness would lift, and the curfew as well. He closed his eyes and buried his hands in his armpits. A few moments later, a man stepped out of the shadows, glanced up and down the empty avenue, and got in the car. He muttered a greeting and gave an address on the other side of town. With a nod, they were off.

These people, whoever they were, always seemed like ghosts to Fernando. They shared many things, one might suspect, but nothing they could talk about. There was an unreality to this existence, floating from house to house. The art of clandestine life was to be invisible, to leave no trace. Fernando only saw it from the outside, these predawn drives through the backstreets of Lima, a morose stranger in the seat beside him. He could imagine the rooms where they stayed: the bare white walls, the single bed and thin mattress, the creaky chair. He had promised Maruja he would never do it. He had a daughter now, and the thought of that life made him sick. Fernando gripped the steering wheel tightly.

There were no traffic lights at this hour, or at least none that anyone paid attention to. The city was shuttered and asleep. The car rattled noisily. The man took off his knit cap and rubbed his face. He pulled a pack of cigarettes from an inside pocket and offered one to Fernando. They smoked and said nothing. There was no one out, not a soul. The radio had been stolen a few months before, but Fernando had never missed it as much as he did now: a song, a voice, anything to erase this quiet. He ran through a handful of questions in his mind—How long were you at the old house? Do you know José Carlos? Where will you go next?—but they were all wrong. He couldn't ask anything like that. Nice sweater, Fernando nearly said, where did you get it? He was embarrassed by the thought. Was it allowed? Talking about clothes? Soccer? The weather?

"It's cold," Fernando offered.

"Sure is."

It was a terrible life. Fernando felt afraid, as if his passenger were not an anonymous comrade, but the victim of an unnamable illness. Something contagious. He felt revulsion. What did *comrade* mean anyway? Who was this man? He wanted him out of his car, the errand over. He wanted to be home, next to his wife and child, asleep again, away from the misery this man carried with him.

They hadn't spoken for blocks when the man said, "Oh, I know this street." He asked Fernando to stop at the corner.

"This isn't the place."

"Just for a moment." The man turned to him. "Please."

Fernando let the car slow.

"Here," the man said and rolled his window down. The air was cool and damp.

"What are we looking at?" Fernando asked.

The man pointed at a nondescript building across the street. It had a high, rusty fence, the kind a house thief would sneer at. The curtains were drawn, and there were no lights. "Someone you know?" Fernando asked.

"Sure."

They sat like that for a moment. The man was sailing, he was dreaming. Fernando could see it: that despairing look of a man confronted with his vanished life. "Do you want to get out?" Fernando asked.

"Not especially."

"Then we should go," Fernando said after a moment. The spell was broken.

The man shook his head. "That's right, *compadre*," he said. "We should go." He sighed and pulled out another cigarette. This time he didn't offer. "I knew a girl there. Once."

"How long has it been?"

"Since she died."

They rode on. The man left his window down. Fernando didn't complain about the cold. He pushed the gas and the engine groaned. It would be morning soon.

IV. Mother, 1984

These were the days when his mother was dying. She had in fact stopped living several years before, when her husband passed away. Fernando just out of the university. The children huddled together in Lima, and, over the course of three nights of drinking and storytelling, forgave the old man everything. Fernando's mother sat on her own, alternately accepting and rejecting her children's affections. She had already done her forgiving, of course, but dying was his last betrayal. She moved to her daughter's house, where they made up a small room for her. It had a window looking out on a quiet street, and a terrace where she sat if it wasn't too cold. But she missed him. She confessed to Fernando that she couldn't remember what her life had been like before his father. Grief exposed all her weaknesses and showed her strengths for what they were: circumstance coupled with faith. She fell into dreams. She lost her faith.

"I'll be dead soon," she told her son, but nearly seven years passed this way and she was still alive. She began to forget. In the afternoons, in deep concentration, she sat down to drink her soup, cradling the bowl in her lap with a napkin spread primly across her thin legs. She smiled and nodded her head in greeting on Sundays when Fernando came to see her, but her smile was civil rather than warm. At times, she felt her family's eyes on her and wished that she could disappear. Other days, her daughter's children played in her room and told her jokes that made her laugh. She had to smile at their friendly disposition, even if she wondered who they might be.

Fernando still came by, but his visits were short. He could squeeze in a drink with his brother-in-law, but never two, and tried to be discreet when he looked at his watch over the rim of the raised glass.

There was hardly any time for socializing. Fernando felt weak. He often woke up dizzy, aching, unable to move, as if sleep, having let his mind go free, were jealously refusing to relinquish his body. He kept his eyes closed tightly, trying to blink away the pains that gripped his body. Unable to sleep, unable to wake, he lay on the bed immobile. Maruja worried about him. He wouldn't let anyone see him this way except her. She wrapped ice in an old shirt and pressed it to his forehead. By midmorning, his fever had cooled, and Fernando could stand, slowly. Once he was up, he wouldn't stop moving until the late evening, when, after telling others there was no time to rest and that the time to act was now, he would lie down to sleep, worried and brooding. The war had been killing him for a long time before he died.

This was not the man his mother would have remembered, if within her clouded memory, something had sparked a moment of lucidity. If she could have recalled Fernando, she would have described a young man who made strangers feel instantly comfortable.

"He was a Boy Scout in Arequipa, and an altar boy at the little church on the Plaza San Antonio de Miraflores. We lived in the little house on Tarapacá and walked to church every Sunday." His comrades called him *Negro*, but in the family he was *Nano*, her youngest child, the one who cost her the most heartache and confusion. He had studied at Independencia, like his older brothers, and years later he still sang his alma mater's hymn proudly, fighting sleep with song as he struggled to stay awake on the eighteen-hour drive back to Arequipa from Lima. He told his mother that melody was unforgettable: *En tus aulas se forjaron grandes hombres . . .* In your halls, great men were molded. He had come to Lima, entertaining little hope of being accepted to the university to study engineering. His older brothers and sister had come before him: Oscar, to the army. Elías, to study accounting. Mateo, to the national police. Enrique, to study medicine. Inés, to study pharmacology. His mother would have remembered the way she saw Fernando off at the bus station, the little bag he carried, his unconcerned smile. It was early morning at the bus station, the first shades of purple sky announcing morning in the east; Padre Alfredo, the priest, a family friend, came to see him off, to wish him luck. His mother would have remembered how sad she was to see her youngest go that morning, how she wondered what she would occupy her day with now, if not waiting for little Nano to come home.

That first year in the city, he sent letters home nearly every week. He had refused to live with his brother or sister, wanting to strike out on his own. Of course they sent him money from Arequipa, which he acknowledged gratefully in his letters. His correspondence was full of a young man's awe at living alone, with enthusiastic descriptions of his boardinghouse in Barrios Altos, of the crowded neighborhood with its teeming street life, panegyrics to Lima and the opportunities it seemed to promise. These were letters that Fernando would have been embarrassed to read later, but his mother had held them nearly sacred at the time. Of course both had forgotten them, and perhaps this was just as well.

She might have remembered his childhood friends, his crew of mischievous, quick-witted boys, nearly all of whom made their way to Lima eventually. If Fernando had ever brought José Carlos around to see her, it might have jogged something in her memory—an image, a flicker. The two boys had been inseparable. She'd found them once, not even eight years old, discussing with great seriousness the creation of a superhero who would be a combination of the two of them, an amalgam of their unique virtues. She had lingered in the doorway, listening, laughing to herself. Having humbly appraised their various qualities, the two boys had left the most contentious topic for last: a name for their conqueror.

All this was forgotten, along with a hundred other details, moments, words: she had never thought much of his politics, had avoided the room whenever the heated talk began between father and son. The boy had opinions on everything. She hadn't wanted to notice when his letters took on a different tenor: his new obsession was Lima and its poverty. One long note was spent describing the trials of a destitute newspaper vendor, a wizened man who claimed to carry his meager life savings in a pouch around his neck. He'd lost his family in a landslide, Fernando wrote, but the man held on. He walked to Lima. No one had come to help them. Fernando found it horrifying, or at least his letters said so.

His mother found it appalling as well. "There are poor right here!" she exclaimed as her husband read the letter aloud. She felt pity for Fernando then: he was such a sensitive boy, to let other people's problems upset him so.

Now she was dying. Inés called one Sunday to tell him this fact. She was older than Fernando by eight years, and liked to make that clear. He had been promising to come visit for weeks, had meant to. "Honestly," he said.

"You don't remember us. You don't come around, Nano. Meanwhile your own mother—"

Fernando cut her off. It was early morning, a Sunday. In better times, he might have come by that afternoon, taken Inés's sons to play soccer in the park, filled up the station wagon with Maruja's boys too and made a day of it. Through his bedroom window, he could see the sun peeking through the fog. Maruja sat at the foot of the bed, her hair wet, pulling on a pair of jeans and a sweater. It was the last time he spoke with his sister for over a year. He would remember it clearly. Inés was excitable, given to waves of sentimentality that could come at any time: a mention of Arequipa, a song, an old picture tugging at her heart from behind a dirty glass frame. But her mother—nothing and no one was more sacred or more special than her mother, who had raised her and guided her. "Fernando, we owe her everything."

"Inés, Inésita. *Cálmate . . .*"

His head hurt each morning in a new way. Sometimes the dizziness overcame the pounding, sometimes his body shook with such force that he wondered if others could see he was falling apart. But to Inés, he was whole, composed. He spoke quietly but did not waver.

"Our mother has everything. She has a home to sleep in. She has food to eat. She has a family to care for her. What about the other mothers? The ones who have nothing? Who will visit them?"

"Their children."

"Their children are busy," he said. "They're cleaning your house."

"Go to hell, Nano. I don't need your lectures."

"I can't come today."

"You're cruel." She hung up the phone softly.

V. Father, 1966

Fernando placed first in the national exam. He was admitted to the university. It came so suddenly, such good news so unexpectedly, that his parents drove to Lima to congratulate him. They met at Elías's house, the family gathering around to toast Fernando, their youngest. His unruly black hair had been shaved down to the scalp. It made him look even younger than he was, seventeen, but it was tradition. Around Lima, on the buses and in the streets, you could spot the bald young men who had just been accepted. At the party, everyone made fun of his bald head. The photos show Fernando smiling happily, his arms slung over his brothers' shoulders, with Mateo's large hands curling over his younger brother's scalp and onto his forehead. Everyone is laughing in the photograph, including Enrique behind tinted frames, and Elías, the oldest, whose smile was a replica of his father's.

Fernando made a toast, to the coming challenges, to his chosen profession, engineering, and to all the people without homes whom he planned to build houses for. There were chuckles all around, but not from Fernando. He meant every word.

And there was no laughter from his father, Don José, who perhaps knew his son best. Fernando, who argued but always listened. Fernando, who threatened his family with his failure just to remind them he was independent. Fernando, who at age four, undersized and quiet, had refused to eat another bite—not for his mother, not for his sister, and not for his brother. "Who will you eat for, Nano?"

"For Guminga," he said emphatically. "For Gu-min-ga."

Dominga, the maid. Even then he was with the people, Don José thought. Dominga was a child herself when she first came to the house, barely eighteen, taking care of the home, cooking, cleaning, and looking after the infant Fernando. She was the first maid the family had been able to afford. Now Dominga lived in a small room, next to the kitchen. She had sewn a curtain out of scraps of fabric and hung it from a rod above the door. If a candle came down the hallway in the middle of the night, she would sit up in bed, peering out into the kitchen to see if she was needed. She was from Puno, from the cold altiplano, where she went every August on her two-week vacation. She wore her hair in two even braids that stretched to the center of her back. Not beautiful, not even pretty, she had an oval face and inky black eyes. Still, the simplicity of her desires gave her an air of satisfaction that others spend their lives chasing. A bed, a roof, a little money to send home; that was all, and when she held Fernando, she was somewhere altogether different, and there was nothing ordinary about her life because she was wanted. Don José had seen her, and it amazed him: the child could do that to her, with his searching look, with his conviction that she stand by him, and be near him, before he drifted into sleep. Even now she had sent a small tin of jam wrapped in newspaper, a present, she said, for the young engineer. She still remembered him. "Little Nano," she had said to Don José. "Give him a kiss for me."

Don José, watching his son toast the houses he would build for Peru's homeless, watching his son tremble with emotion at the warmth of the family surrounding him, recognized that Fernando's heart was like his own: nostalgic but combative, caring but suspicious, able to bundle great ideas into intractable knots of personal anxiety. It is the way men begin to carry the world with them, the way they become responsible for it, not through their minds, but through their hearts. And though they shared much, the differences between Don José and his son were also striking, and also a question of heart. Don José saw that as well and did not, as others did, attribute those differences to something as simple as youth.

Don José, as a young man, had been a Communist. It was easy and logical. His brothers and sisters had all taken the well-worn paths that life in the provinces afforded them. Ricardo and Jaime were farm workers and spent their days bent over in fields they did not own. Luis worked in a leather shop, crafting saddles and belts, bags and soccer balls. By the time Fernando entered high school his uncle Luis was nearly blind. Don José's sisters had never had schooling beyond the fifth grade. They had married young, become the kinds of women who tended to their husbands' houses without complaint or worry. They shopped every morning for that day's meals and went to the plaza to have their letters read to them. Life was work. Life was spent living. Don José read books, studied, became a schoolteacher, and eventually a principal. He loved, he married, and he strayed. Mateo, Fernando's half brother, came to live with the family when he was five. Don José found himself, now the gentleman he had always imagined he could be, disappointed in himself, in his lack of drive and desire. Fernando carried within him those qualities that time had conspired to take from his father.

One must understand what it means to be born at the foot of a volcano. Arequipa is less a city than a living temple to El Misti, that imposing mass of rock rising behind the cathedral. Men invoke its name to describe what is right. What does a volcano do to a man but impress upon him the need to dream on a grand scale?

In 1950, when Fernando was two years old, Independencia went on strike. The students closed the doors of the school, locked themselves inside to protest the raising of school fees. Three tense days followed, with skirmishes along the fences and students pulling stones from the courtyard to throw at police. The government sent in the army, a student was killed. The city took to the streets. Every man in Arequipa knew that if the cathedral's bell was ringing, it was time to rally in the square. The city's narrow lanes filled with angry townspeople, farmers, ranchers, merchants, students. In Arequipa, you had a right to be angry. You had a right to demand better: didn't their volcano prove that they were destined for much more? And people listened: as Arequipa went on strike, other cities and towns across Peru followed suit. The crisis came and power changed hands. The stage shifted. If only for a day, a week, a month, those in power were forced to listen to the people. This was how things got done. This was tradition.

The party rose to a boil. Someone had dusted off a guitar, and Mateo was threatening to sing. He had returned from a trip north, bronzed and happy, telling stories of Ecuadorian girls and nights on the beach. Enrique was dancing with Inés, chiding his sister for her lack of rhythm. Don José felt a warmth in his chest, the comforting sensation that everything was going to be fine; that his work, if such a thing existed, was nearly done. He wasn't old, not yet, but look at what he had accomplished! His children stood before him in diverse stages of drunken cheer, and they all seemed like the kind of people he'd like, if he were to meet them as strangers on a train station platform or in a European café. He had raised them well, or his wife had, or maybe they had done it together—but still: he hadn't ruined them! Don José felt like weeping: his children were the sort of people who would make something out of this country, who could redeem this mess they'd inherited. He wanted to touch their faces, to show them off to the world. Could they be real?

Someone called for a toast. The room had the flickering warmth of a silent movie, except suddenly Don José was talking, the words, he feared, pouring forth without poetry, without grace. He was forced to admit he'd lost count of the drinks. His loved ones laughed with him. Fernando stood with his mother, their hands clasped tightly. She had missed him most this year. It was terrible to see her this way, Don José thought. Watching their son from afar held no pleasure for her: she couldn't appreciate the spectacle the way Don José could. Now, their youngest nearly a man, and look at her: holding his hand like a child, and Nano, generous-hearted, letting her.

He was a beautiful boy.

When he finished, Don José found a place on the sofa, a comfortable position from which to gaze at his family. An hour passed and the liquor ran out. Inés apologized, smirking. "I didn't prepare for you hooligans."

Mateo consoled a red-faced Fernando, shouting in his ear as if he were hard of hearing, "No more liquor? It's all right, Nano, we'll drink vinegar!"

To Don José's surprise, his wife joined him after a while. She brought him coffee and sat close to him, their thighs touching for the first time in many months. He took her hand and raised it to his lips. She blushed. Someone was singing—off-key, out of tune—did it matter? Don José kissed his wife's hand softly.

VI. Pinochet's Graveyard, 1973

In December of 1973, José Carlos arrived from Santiago de Chile, thin, broken, with hands that shook uncontrollably. He stumbled over his words and brooded in long silences, looking away into the distance, the ash from his cigarette floating into his lap.

"They killed me, Negro, they killed me," he said, his voice trembling. Fernando met him at the airport; José Carlos staggered off the last airlift of Peruvian citizens from Chile. The rest stayed to die.

"Where did they keep you?"

"In Pinochet's graveyard, in the stadium. We had nothing to defend ourselves with."

The story came out slowly, over many nights. José Carlos was smaller and weaker than Fernando remembered. His movements came haltingly: a finger rubbing his temples, a foot tapping an uneven rhythm. Five years at the university in Santiago. José Carlos had been expelled without papers, without a degree, with nothing.

"What did they do to you, José Carlos?"

"They killed me. They kept us in the stadium. There were thousands of us. I was locked in a dressing room under the stands with two hundred others, mostly students. Communists. They kept the lights on, fluorescent lights, burning our eyes. We slept in groups, took turns standing. Twelve hours at a time, standing with people I'd never met before and others I knew well. It was impossible to sleep. We heard shots sometimes from outside. People were dragged out screaming and never came back. They pulled me out too. I was angry. You're going to die, you piece of shit. *Comunista*. They spat on me. Peruvian dog, you're going to die in Chile today! I told them to go to hell. They were young, the soldiers, just children, but cold. They wouldn't look me in the eye. I remember one of the officers: he was silent, standing behind. He had big hands. Finally, he yelled out, Tie him up, and they did. They put my hands behind my back and then blindfolded me. I spat at them. Say your last words, Communist. Fuck off, I said. I'm ready."

José Carlos spilled the ashtray with a clumsy brush of his arm; he was shaking violently. Fernando moved quickly to sweep the ash into his hands.

"They shot me, Negro! They killed me!" José Carlos brought his hand down hard against the table, slapping it loudly. "They shot me with blanks! They played at killing me!"

"They dragged me back to the dressing room. I smelled from my own piss and shit. My friends there held me. Someone threw water on me. You're alive, they said, but I didn't believe them. No bullet touched you, they said, but I knew I had felt it. I spent three days dead, Fernando. Three days . . ."

José Carlos's voice was thin and smoky. "That's what they're going to do to you."

"What do we do, *Perucho*?" Fernando took his hand and squeezed. "You're home. We're alive."

José Carlos shook his head, and coughing loudly, put out his cigarette. "It's simple, Negro. The side with guns always wins."

VII. To Lima, 1965

Then there was the bus that took Fernando to Lima. It was the kind of contraption held together by ingenuity, built from salvaged parts with the practiced art of making do. Learn what the engine can handle and disregard its feelings, its wishes, and its whims.

Repairs were cruel surgeries of convenience, and the bus grew hardened, indifferent, and ran from spite and disgust, crossing Andean passes, wheezing and cursing the broad-bowed freighter that brought it from Germany, the United States, or Sweden. Soon the seats were cracked and choking with dust, the windows rattled with each bump, each pothole, each patch of rough stones. The passengers rode, somehow coaxing sleep from the nauseating pounding of metal and glass, and the murderous odors of diesel.

This is how Fernando came to Lima at age seventeen: wearing a brown sweater over a modest button-up, with blue slacks and black shoes worn thin at the heels. Riding that bus, seated in the back row with six others, a mishmash collection of souls on one or another of life's various errands: to buy, to sell, to visit, to marry, to find, and more than a few, to forget.

Young people climbed onto the bus in the dead of night, leaving behind bankrupt and miserable villages of adobe houses and cold fields of cotton and maize. They carried a change of clothes, a picture, a little food, a plastic comb, a letter of introduction, a bag of coca leaves, or a crucifix. They dropped their bundles in the aisle and stood for twelve hours, until the sun was up and roaring, the bus warm and drowsy with heat, and still they stood, beads of sweat forming on their lips and on their temples. Fernando watched them. They were his contemporaries. His countrymen. He watched them pull a few soles from their pockets, haggle with the driver, shake their heads, and point their fingers. Their skin toughened by the sun and the wind. Some spoke only Quechua and some seemed not to speak at all.

Sometime in the afternoon the driver lost control. In a frightening half-second, the tires slid on the gravel, the road slipping beneath them. With a punishing blow, the bus slammed into the side railing, swerved back toward the mountain, toward safety, and came to rest, half-leaning, half-balancing against the brittle and crumbling earth that overlooked the road. To their right, just beyond the guardrail, a jagged drop-off and the valley below. People picked themselves up slowly. Bags and blankets were pushed aside. Fernando found himself stretched across three strangers. Legs and arms sorted themselves out. Mothers attended to crying children. Someone handed him his glasses with a smile and asked if he was all right. Everyone seemed to be reasonably well, though shaken—except the driver, who had taken it worst of all, perhaps because he had seen that shocking flash of blue across his window as the bus peered over the edge. He knew better than anyone how close they had come. The force of the accident had thrown him from his seat, but he had climbed back up to his perch, pulled the door release, and then sat still, pallid, gripping the wheel, rocking his head back and forth, eyes glazed, reliving the accident. A few people stopped to check on him, to pat him on the shoulder, to urge him outside, but he ignored them.

The men, with Fernando eagerly helping, set about the business of righting the bus. It was leaning precariously against the dirt rock wall of the road, its right tires about two or three feet off the ground. The cargo tied to the racks on the roof of the bus had come loose. Now it draped over the edge of the right-side windows. The tarp that covered the cargo had held, the suitcases, sacks, and crates together still, but dangling dangerously from the top of the bus.

Fernando walked to the edge where the bus had nearly taken flight and looked out over the valley. It was a tremendous sight, a magnificent Andean landscape, a silver-gray sheath of rock, a fierce blue sky, and along the hills, footpaths where man and beast walked. Perhaps the Inca's own messengers had marched along those paths in the days before the Spanish, before

Atahualpa tossed Pizarro's Bible to the ground, before the killing began. There was a spectacular loneliness in the mountains, in the grand theater of wind and sky, mountain and water, and so much quiet, Fernando felt ashamed to speak. Perhaps he imagined this, or imposed it on himself, or perhaps he adopted the quiet rectitude of his fellow passengers, who nodded and gestured more than they spoke. Fernando longed to know their language.

Then the driver, still shaken, stepped into the sun-struck day, pointing frantically at the luggage compartment beneath the coach. And suddenly they heard it—the banging, clawing against metal, a sound previously lost in the wind. The men sprang into action, and in an instant, the door was open, and beneath luggage and crates, a man emerged. He had been asleep beneath the bus, having driven all night, waiting to replace the driver at the next town. They pulled him out, his legs kicking, arms flailing, a man being born again, having experienced death blindly.

"Brother," the driver said, rushing toward him. "My brother!"

Fernando could hear the man breathing, pulling in enormous lungs full of oxygen, replenishing himself. The man was crying and fearful. "Oh God, Oh God, Oh God," he murmured. A thin stream of blood curled from his bottom lip. The brothers embraced and Fernando fell in love with his people.

VIII. Carmen, 1986

His mother died. Lima accepted his sadness and gave him a month of sunless days. At the funeral, Fernando held Inés's hand. The war had worsened. It seemed that the city might fall at any moment. In Lima, people tried to live their lives as if nothing were happening, but no one slept by the windows anymore. Bombs could go off at any moment. Fathers rushed home to beat the curfew. Young people used it as an excuse to stay out all night. Parties had devolved into fatalistic bacchanals.

Sixteen journalists were killed in a faraway mountain village. The peasants had mistaken them for collaborators. News crawled into Lima ten days later. In San Martín, a group of rebels took over a jungle town and waved rifles in the air. Guerrilla leaders, drunk with victory, pulled bandanas from their faces and announced to television cameras that victory was near. A shocked nation stared at its tormentors. The papers called them terrorists. In Lima, Fernando cringed. A backlash would come soon.

On July 13, 1986, Carmen was born on the third floor of the public hospital in central Lima.

With Carmen, Fernando and Maruja were finally alive. It was as if they had been sleeping all along. He had never seen anyone more beautiful than Maruja that morning she gave birth to his child, and when Carmen slept for the first time on his chest, he felt complete. Even as he held her, he realized he was placing a wager on his life: that the war might not spare him long enough to see her grow. Still at the hospital, he confided with Maruja that he was afraid. She said that she had always been.

Carmen was an accident. Maruja had never been convinced, not until that moment that she held the child and discovered that she could love that much again. She told Fernando that she hadn't expected to find that within her once more. Fernando's health reappeared, and he carried Carmen with him everywhere.

He relished changing her diapers. He rode the bus with his daughter asleep on his lap. In meetings, while comrades waved fingers and spoke forcefully, Fernando rocked the child and whispered nursery rhymes in her ear, so she wouldn't be afraid of the loud voices.

Maruja brought home a map one day, and they tacked it to their bedroom wall. That evening, once the baby was asleep, they stood hand in hand to marvel at the size of the world. It was comforting to see how little their war was, and to think there were places out there where their struggles were not news.

But in public, they showed no signs of retreat. Maruja stayed with her union. Fernando traveled to the interior and back, lightning trips to visit universities in Piura and union meetings in Huancavelica, returning to Lima on the overnight bus to see his daughter in her crib. His promise—to never leave Lima—was not mentioned.

He took Carmen with him one day when he was called to the home of a murdered syndicalist in San Juan de Lurigancho to offer the Party's condolences. It was daylight and safe, he thought, but he hated this work. The man had lived in that part of the city built of dust. The bus let Fernando off in front of a newspaper stand. It was a warm day, inexplicably sunny. Children in tattered clothing watched Fernando as he passed, while his baby girl slept against his chest, oblivious. He'd been here, to this very home, ages ago, in the dead of night. Fernando had met the murdered man, but no picture came to mind: no toothy smile, no salt-and-pepper hair, no bushy eyebrows or face creased with wrinkles. It worried him. Now he would meet the man's widow, and the prospect of her sadness seemed daunting. He walked on to the house, certain his feet would remember the way. His daughter yawned. Her tiny mouth opening, she blinked, and then fell asleep again. It took only a moment. Her hair had fallen out a few weeks after birth: thin, reddish brown, and straight like her mother's. Fernando held her in his shadow so that the sun wouldn't wake her.

He was walking along a dusty street a few blocks from the bus stop when a boy came toward him with a steady stare. He appeared suddenly from the shadowed doorway of a storefront, as if he'd been waiting. "Hey, mister," he asked, "are you the man from the city?"

He said *city* as if it were far away. Fernando shook his head and walked on.

But the boy insisted. His voice was deep for his size, or maybe he was small for his age. "She's waiting for you. Señora Aronés."

"The widow?"

"My mother," the boy said flatly. He cupped a hand over his eyes. "She said you were coming."

Fernando followed the boy. "How is she?" he asked.

"The house is just over there."

"Is there anything I can do?"

The boy frowned. "Were you his friend?"

"We worked together."

"I'm not stupid, mister." He rubbed his eyes. "You got him killed."

Fernando stood, dumbstruck. The boy didn't back down. His jaw was set fiercely. He hates me, Fernando thought, and the idea shocked him. "You've misunderstood, son."

But the boy didn't answer. Someone from the house had recognized Fernando, was calling his name, "Negro . . ."

"My mother's in there," the boy said grimly and walked away.

The home was surrounded by mourners. Fernando made his way inside, shaking hands on the way with men who recognized him. No one here seemed to blame him. Still, he felt numb. There were more people crowded inside, forming a circle around the widow. Fernando sat on the dirt floor. The widow thanked him for coming without even glancing up at him. When she finally looked up, she nodded. "You've been here before."

"Your husband was a good friend."

Someone brought him a glass of soda and he drank politely. He was there to watch her cry. He was there to show that she hadn't been forgotten.

"Can I hold her?" she asked after a moment. She meant Camucha. The widow's face was flush and red. He looked around her bare home; all her worldly possessions could fit into a trunk. And now she had lost it all. It was there on her face for anyone to see. Her son would never recover. Fernando passed her his sleeping child. Something like a smile graced the widow's lips, flashed for a moment, and was gone.

VIII. La Uni, 1977

At La Uni, they were safe. Inside they could speak their minds, wear their affiliations on their sleeves. Students denounced their professors, stormed out of class and into the streets. Some disappeared into the mountains to learn the art of war. Every wall spoke politics: an angry poster announced a meeting; a slogan appeared, scrawled in red across the bricks. With angry partisans looking on, a frightened groundskeeper painted over it all. He did it every week.

Some hid their entire adult lives in and out of halls of La Uni.

Fernando knew them. One man, Victor, never stayed in a house very long, two weeks but not more, and came to the university with fake papers to meet his comrades. He had left medical school in his second year and spent some time in Cusco with the peasants during the land takeovers. He plowed the earth with the Indians and carried water for their crops in leaky wooden pails. Back in Lima, he threw rocks at the Presidential Palace and broke windows at the Congress building. When the situation allowed, he set fires, and then people began to whisper his name. In 1977, he was already wanted. His friends remarked that the posters made him look even slighter than he was.

Victor fell ill in the early spring. A man came looking for Fernando at La Uni and told him the news. The messenger was paunchy and dark, careful with his words. Each syllable escaped through his teeth, so Fernando was forced to lean close simply to hear him. It was the way people in the movement spoke. "Victor needs a doctor. He says he knows what it is, only he can't operate on himself."

Fernando's brother Enrique was a doctor. He had trained in North America. He would know someone, or he could even see the patient himself. Fernando called him and they met at Inés's house in San Miguel. It was a Saturday afternoon in October. Inés poured drinks while her brothers spoke. Her two boys ran through the living room, screaming and laughing. They attacked their uncles with hugs and jumped into Enrique's lap. "What are you learning in school now, Ciro?"

"Nothing," the boy said, laughing.

"And you, Guillermo?"

"Can't remember."

He was only in first grade, but Fernando was afraid it was true. Public schools in Lima were not like Independencia; they were crowded, chaotic, dirty. Enrique was urging Inés to save for a private school. The boys ran outside to play.

When it was quieter, Fernando told Enrique about Victor. "He's a friend," he said. "He can't go to the hospital."

"Don't ask me to get involved, Nano."

"Involved?" Fernando laughed. "Come on, *hermano*. It's just a small favor."

"I wish I could help."

"It would all be very quiet."

Enrique shook his head. "I'm sorry."

Inés's boys were kicking a deflated plastic ball in front of the house. Ciro waved and smiled through the window, then kicked the ball straight at them. Both Fernando and Enrique flinched, but the ball ricocheted harmlessly off the iron bars in front of the glass. The boys smirked, then Ciro raised his arms and shouted *gol* with such exuberance that Fernando couldn't help but smile.

But Enrique didn't. He turned away from the window.

"Well?" Fernando asked.

"You know what, *hermanito*?" Enrique said in a sharp whisper. "I have a wife. I have two daughters. I have a son on the way."

They had discussed this before, across their father's kitchen table in Arequipa: What will you do when the time comes to act? What is demanded of people like us in a country like this?

"When you're my age you'll understand, Nano."

A radio hummed in the background. They could hear Inés singing along to the old tune from the kitchen. Enrique got up without saying another word. Fernando watched his older brother through the window. Enrique picked up one of the boys and put him on his shoulders. The boy shrieked with delight.

Sometimes Fernando thought they scarcely seemed like brothers at all.

Victor died in a windowless basement apartment in Barrios Altos of complications resulting from acute appendicitis.

X. Mateo, 1989

Fernando stopped by Mateo's apartment one evening. It was November. Soon the city would be beautiful again. The brothers embraced warmly; though they lived nearby, they had not seen each other in months. Fernando sat down, and Mateo brought him a drink. "This apartment is killing me, Nano," he said.

The curtains were drawn. All the furniture was covered in dust. "You changed the arrangement here, no?" Fernando asked.

"We moved everything toward the center. Away from the window," Mateo said, nodding absentmindedly. "Bombs."

Outside, along the avenue, just one hundred feet from Mateo's window, there was a red brick wall that read NO STOPPING UNDER PENALTY OF DEATH. Behind it, there was an army installation. Every two hundred feet or so, a turret stood above the brick wall, each with an armed soldier inside. Mateo had been pleading with the landlord to let his family move to another apartment, one that wasn't so compromised by its location.

The sofa was set in the middle of the room; two strips of electrical tape made an X across each window. "To keep the glass from blowing inward."

Fernando nodded. He had done the same in his apartment. Mateo's neighbors had moved away. "We try not to look out the window," Mateo said, finishing his drink.

"Someone has been watching me, Mateo."

"Of course."

Mateo knew exactly what his brother was involved in. They had never discussed it, but each assumed that they knew the same people, only from different sides. They were right. Mateo was an officer. Policía Nacional del Perú. "What happened?" he asked.

"My car was stolen, the other day, near the university—"

"Which doesn't in itself mean anything."

"No, of course not." Fernando chuckled. "It's a piece of shit, but still, it's surprising it hasn't happened sooner. But what happened after was strange. I reported it to the police. At the station, they made me wait. Then an officer came out, less than two hours after it had gone, and told me they had found my car."

Stolen cars don't appear in Lima, not like that, not until the piranhas have taken them apart. Mateo knew that. Everyone knew that.

Fernando continued. "They took me right to it, right where I had left it. Exactly as it was before I had reported it missing." He paused, and leaned over the table toward Mateo. "Except my briefcase was missing."

"You're certain?"

"Gone."

"Did you go back for it?"

Fernando nodded.

"You shouldn't have." Mateo shook his head. "What did they tell you?"

"'So, it seems you're some kind of *politico,* no?'"

"And you said?"

Fernando paused, taking a deep, tired breath. He hadn't slept. "I said where's my fucking briefcase."

"Nano!" Mateo stood up with a start. "How could you put

yourself in that kind of position? How could you have so little regard for your own life?"

"I don't know. I messed up." He looked down. He wiggled his toes inside his shoes.

"Nano," his brother said. "Look at me. What was in the briefcase? What did you have in there?"

"Documents. Papers. Names. I don't know exactly. Maybe nothing."

"Nothing?"

Fernando was suddenly afraid. "I haven't told Maruja."

"Is she implicated?" Mateo asked.

"No."

"Are you?"

Fernando closed his eyes but didn't answer. Mateo was still standing over him when he opened them again. The brothers stared at each other for a moment, in silence.

Mateo slumped down in his chair again.

"The circle is tightening, Nano. . . . Be careful."

XI. Oxapampa, 1989

A few weeks before Christmas, the Party called on Fernando to make a trip. He didn't tell Maruja where he was going, although she must have suspected. He didn't inform the university that he was taking leave, nor did he expect to be gone for long. Fernando took a bus to Huancayo, and in the noisy bus station he met his contact, a comrade from the Party. Together, they rode away from Huancayo, north into the valley, and then into the jungle. They spent one night in Oxapampa, registered under false names at a local hotel, and woke with flea bites and neck cramps. They hiked for the next two days and then met another man, who led them even farther. And then, in a clearing, three days from anywhere, Fernando met the combatants. José Carlos had been waiting for him.

The fighters were young and frightened and dwarfed by their weapons. They had scarcely begun to live. They had never read Marx or heard of Castro. Some had never been to Lima. There was little bravado among them, little of that swagger that one would associate with carrying a gun. The forest was dark and damp. In camp, they made space for the visitor from Lima in one of the olive green tents. Fernando thought they looked ill, gaunt, tired. He briefly felt shame.

There was a clearing, where the rebels learned the basics of engagement. In the mornings, they dispersed in squadrons, drifting into the jungle; they ran exercises, learned how to use their guns. They hid from one another and shot the branches off trees from a hundred yards away. They tossed rocks at targets, pretending they were grenades. Fernando watched as they threw, counting—one, two, three, four—and whispered the coming explosion:

Boom.

Those who saw him then described Fernando as electric, brilliant, defining the sacrifices that still awaited them, and the injustices that had steeled their resolve. No question animated him more, sparked more passion within him, than why. Why there were no choices; why the time was now; why victory was assured.

It came from his heart, but he spoke with his hands, his arms, his entire body. Why the people had been denied schooling; why their fathers worked land they would never own; why their mothers cleaned houses; why their uncles did not stop working until blindness overwhelmed them. Why the defeated chased happiness in drink; why wealth bred depravity. Why the history was cruel and maniacal; why blood must be shed.

Standing in front of a map of the Americas tacked to the mossy trunk of a jungle tree, Fernando ran his finger up and down the peaks of the Andes, the spine of his continent, and told the tattered and inexperienced group of fighters what he would die believing that very day:

"All of this will be ours once more," he said.

And he smiled as they repeated it with him. He delighted in the sound of their rising voices.

He looked up and caught a glimpse of the swollen sky through the forest's canopy.

"All of this will be ours once more!" he said again.

And the words filled him with an inexplicable joy, even hope.

He was still alive.

a science for being alone

Every year on Mayra's birthday, since she turned one, I have asked Sonia to marry me. This year our little girl turned five. Each rejection has its own story, but until recently, before the two of them left, I preferred to think of these moments as one long, unfinished conversation. Mayra's fifth fell on a hot, bright day. I had twenty-five soles in my pocket, the ring, and a little makeup kit I'd bought for my daughter. I was at the Plaza Manco Capac, waiting for a spot at the lunch counter of a cheap criollo place before heading over to see the women of my life.

Sonia and Mayra lived in a hostel downtown. It's an old building that belonged to the man who would have been my father-in-law. When Sonia failed the university exam, her father sent her to the States to learn a little of the language of tourism. When she returned he installed her in the hostel as the administrator. Mayra was just a few months old. The inn is called Hostal New Lima, just like that, with Spanglish syntax. She got the adventurous, the young and unshaven, the backpackers in their inimitable style, wearing vests with dozens of pockets or pants that unzip to become parachutes or inflatable rafts. Americans and Germans and French. For years Sonia occasionally took one to bed, but I never thought these flings amounted to much. In a way, I was proud of our modern arrangement, which I thought approximated those slippery, ambiguous, but ultimately loving relationships I'd seen on American sitcoms. We had our special anniversaries, our traditions, and Mayra's birthday was one of them. It was the day we pretended we were a family still or that we once had been. It was the day I proposed with subtle fanfare that we become one.

The street was steaming, everywhere that soggy and unpleasant heat the city is known for. The plaza was brimming with the destitute and their predators. A man in dirty clothes slept facedown in a sparse patch of grass beneath a tree, while an orange-clad municipal worker swept around him with a large palm frond. At the corner, a few red-eyed street kids huddled greedily around a bag of glue. A woman pushed a cart of bananas up and down the street, her open hand indicating they were five for fifty cents. The bananas were leftovers, throwaways, mushy and bruised and sweet. Peels littered the cracked sidewalk. It was Lima in her splendor. Since being laid off from the bank, I was experiencing for the first time real poverty, distinct from any other I had previously survived. It manifested itself first as a condition of the mind: an emptying panic, a kind of vertigo, coupled with the conviction that all my misfortunes were an elaborate hoax. This set of psychological symptoms is common among those of us who, as children, never had to skip a meal. For us, the current crisis is particularly cruel.

An economist friend of mine said he could always tell how grim the situation was by keeping track of the hours hookers put in. He lived in Lince, near Avenida Arequipa, no more than ten blocks from that notorious strip that's always highlighted on the Sunday television news magazines. In the early 1990s, he said, they didn't appear on the streets till eight or eight-thirty, and disappeared by four. As the crisis deepened, prostitutes worked longer hours, choosing their corners as early as six and staying until the beginnings of the morning rush. A full twelve hours, my friend said, smiling, just like the rest of us.

I recalled this conversation because there in the plaza, just after noon, a middle-aged woman with dyed blond hair was putting in her time too. She was thick and square, her exact age hidden beneath layers of makeup. The meat of her thighs pressed against the fabric of her skirt. Hookers working day shifts, I thought with a laugh, and wondered if my friend could theorize about that level of misery, and then wondered for a moment if he too had been laid off, and if so, what his plans were. Or did he, like me, have none? I watched the woman, her forced coquettish smiles. She perked up pathetically when she saw me glancing at her. I turned away. She'd do better business at dusk, I thought, not in the bright glare of midday.

I was—and I can't explain why exactly—moved by the sight of her. I make no claims to altruism, or to a generosity beyond what is humane and decent. Only this: I felt that something special was in order, something that might make the city more livable, less cruel, softer. It is something maybe any father would feel, on his daughter's birthday or on any day when that child you love helplessly is present in your thoughts, and you wonder what you can do for them or for the world they will inherit. I am also a man whose actions do not always conform to any logic. Sonia used to call me the King of the Desert because of my admiration of the grandiose. I have read history. The hopeless acts of our Peruvian heroes are beautiful in their way, even triumphant. I know our traditions.

We've all had our troubles. My father flirted with bankruptcy for decades before finally giving in. He owned a little bookshop in Miraflores, had flush times and then bad times and then worse times. He sold calendars and notebooks and dictionaries and pencils, and also the classics in leather-bound volumes. By the time the business went under, I was already at the public university and somewhat insulated from my family's troubles. He took work as a cabbie and died a few years after the bank had foreclosed on him. I started helping with an uncle who delivered Mary Kay cosmetics to pharmacies around Lima. We worked the city end to end. This is how I learned to fear poverty.

I bought a handful of bananas, gave up my spot in line, and walked toward the prostitute. She stood under the awning of a photo store, next to a leathery old man selling newspapers spread on a blanket. She saw me coming and smiled. I held my bananas out for her and said hello.

"Hello," she said, smiling conspiratorially. Her face was broad and bronzed by the summer sun. Three freckles dotted her left cheek and rose in unison when she smiled. She looked at her naked wrist. "Is it time, baby?" she asked coyly. "Already?"

"Yes," I said awkwardly.

She frowned, then caught herself. She was younger than I had first thought, not quite forty yet.

I held out the bananas. They were streaked with black. She took the bruised fruit and stroked the length of one of the bananas.

"Ooh, kinky," she said, still smiling. "Do you like kinky, *flaco*?"

The corner was draped in white light. Her faux-blond hair shone carmine against the black roots, then orange, a shifting shade each time she turned her head. With her red fingernails, she pulled one of the bananas from the rest and peeled it lazily, wearing an alternately pained and then delighted expression. She asked me if I liked it. Her three freckles danced.

The blood boiled hot in my ears. I mumbled an apology. She looked at me, uncomprehending, and continued to mime sexy for me, as if by sheer persistence she could arouse me.

There are moments—and I've learned to recognize them—when something that previously seemed quite reasonable, even kind, is revealed to be profoundly stupid. Time stops, words peter out, thoughts shrivel and collapse upon themselves. I'd done this before. Misguided acts of charity. Sometimes I am right and other times I am wrong. I'm never exactly sure what seemingly good idea might entrance me.

An instant later, a police officer had joined our discussion.

"What's going on here?"

"Este pendejo," the woman began, and I knew that whatever she told him would mean bad things for me. She rambled. I had propositioned her, she said, and that wasn't her line of work. It was an insult to her dignity. She was a mother of two and a Christian, she said, pointing at the silver cross that hung in the curve between her breasts. I had been dirty, had insinuated acts that went against nature. She held the bananas up as evidence of my perverse appetites. "I'm only glad you came when you did," she said to the officer. "There's no telling what he might have done."

It was a disgusting display. A middle-aged woman, with children back at the hovel she called home, hooking on a hot February afternoon and turning a simple gift into an excommunicable offense. The cop smelled a shakedown and could barely contain his glee. He sized me up. I hadn't lost the habit of wearing a suit every day. He must have thought I had money. He dismissed the hooker with a nod and a pat on the ass. She sauntered off, turning only to scowl at me. Halfway down the block she let a banana peel slip from her hands into the gutter.

The cop smiled openly now, treacherously. He ran his hands through his oily hair and grabbed me by the arm. His untrimmed fingernails dug into my bicep.

"Let's go for a walk," he said.

Sonia was a student of mine at an admissions prep institute. By the time she had failed the exam the second time, we were already lovers. A year later, at twenty-one, she was pregnant with Mayra. We were unmarried with no intentions. In fact, I never had the chance to ask her. In the same breath she told me she was pregnant and too young to be married. I had just turned twenty-nine and felt too young as well. A scandal ensued. Our parents, who despised each other, met to negotiate. They decided to force us to marry. Decency and decorum were invoked. I went home every night to be berated for my irresponsibility. Sonia was threatened with trials of all kinds. The brutish and short life of our bastard child was described for us in vivid, apocalyptic detail.

One day her father, Mr. Sepulveda, called and said he wanted to speak with me man to man. I came at the appointed hour, nervous in my best suit. I was prepared to be bent and pressured, my will molded anew, certain I would cave. Sonia's mother let me in and asked me to sit. The room was so still and silent I could hear the dust motes settling on the plastic couch covers. Mr. Sepulveda appeared, carrying a tray with two glasses of rum and Coke. He nodded and sat, raising his glass in my direction, before sipping his drink. "A toast," he said obscurely, "to love and to the sea."

"Well," he said, after a sufficiently long pause. "You really fucked up, didn't you?"

"Sir?"

"Did you suppose I asked you here to offer my congratulations?" He shook his head, as if answering his own question, then raised his arms, addressing the ceiling, or perhaps the heavens themselves. "Who am I to blame for all this?"

"I don't know," I said.

Mr. Sepulveda had a grizzled look about him. Sonia, I remember thinking, was beautiful in spite of her father's genes. He was in the process of aging poorly. There was a clumsiness to his features, as if he'd been assembled by a child. When he took a drink the entire glass disappeared in his enormous hands.

"What are your plans then?" he asked. "How will you provide for my grandson?"

I told him I was working at the bank, that I was hoping for a promotion. When I mentioned that I would continue to teach for extra income, he chortled.

"Teaching? That's what you call it? Preying on young women?" he said. "Sonia didn't pass the exam, so what exactly do you teach?"

Sonia is not a test taker. It came down to this simple fact: a fluttering in her heart, perspiration welling up on her palms, all the things she knew fleeing from her. The very words scrambled, she said. It was like being drugged.

I told Mr. Sepulveda the statistics: how fifty thousand apply for seven thousand slots.

"A failed man is never alone," he said sternly. "You know I won the visa lottery?" His gaze tightened on me.

Luck, conveniently reinterpreted as achievement. I nodded.

"I worked with these!" he said, leaning toward me across the coffee table, suddenly animated, holding those large hands in my face. "In Paterson, *Nueva Jersey*, in *Los Uniteds*! With Dominicans! With Puerto Ricans! With blacks! They have children twice a year, those Americans! With fathers who come home from prison on the weekends! Their lives move faster than ours. They murder each other for welfare money! Their children are born addicted to drugs!"

I was starting to have no idea what he was talking about. I nodded only because I didn't know what else to do. Sonia had recounted these diatribes for me with such uncanny accuracy that I felt like he was reading a script. I stifled the urge to smile.

"I've seen it all," he said, falling back into his seat. "What you and my daughter have done. Nothing surprises me anymore. I can't be shocked. Those people."

He pronounced the words as if the very syllables were dirty.

"I don't trust you," he said, "but I trust my daughter."

"I do too, sir."

"Whose idea was it to *not* get married?"

"Ours," I answered.

"Sonia says it was hers."

"Maybe it was hers."

"But you agree?"

I said that I did.

"I would like to kill her, honestly. It's not that I like you, I don't. But still, I would like to force her to marry you." He sighed through his teeth, emitting a thin whistle. "But I won't."

"Sir?"

He asked me how old I was and I told him.

"And where do you work again?"

"At the Inter-Provincial Bank of Peru."

He scanned me from top to bottom. "I can't pretend to understand. I mean, there's nothing obviously wrong with you." He emptied his rum and Coke. "You can wait a while, can't you?"

I nodded, though I wasn't exactly sure what I was agreeing to, or what had just transpired. I didn't dare smile, or betray any expression, and in any case, I wasn't even sure what I felt: Relief? Disappointment? Confusion? Was I being blocked from marrying the woman I loved or had I been spared the consequences of a youthful indiscretion? He looked at me for a moment longer and sighed once more. Sonia's mother reappeared in the doorframe.

"Well, son," Mr. Sepulveda said. "Go ahead and finish your drink. I have work to do."

The cop led me to a desolate corner of the neighborhood, where the cobblestones shone through the crumbling cement like open wounds. My shoes were scuffed and worn at the toes; his were polished a midnight black. I tried reasoning with him, but explanations were useless, equivocations beside the point. My daughter, Mayra, the collapsing economy, my protestations of poverty—all superfluous details. Starting at thirty, he worked his way down in increments of five soles. He described my humiliation, the effect an arrest for solicitation might have on my attempts to return to the world of finance. He murmured encouragement. He lathered himself in generosity. He saluted the flag. It was an outrageous bribe, an unheard-of sum, but I paid ten soles just to be done with him. If he'd wanted more, if he'd wanted Sonia's ring or Mayra's gift, I was prepared to fight him, I told myself, no matter the consequences.

The day was already long, though it was barely past two. I walked back toward downtown, commiserating with myself, creating and then debunking excuses for my own buffoonery. We are a nation of skillful gesturists. Men and women who transcend with small actions, a people condemned to make poetry. I am no different, working gracelessly within that grand tradition. Our heroes ride their steeds off mountain bluffs, tumbling to glorious deaths. They inject themselves with poisons and languish in the name of medical progress. Inevitably our heroes die, or their hopes do, and this is a plaintive point of pride for our long-suffering people. How and when, the method and the moment for a final and solitary defeat. It is our highest art.

Mayra was born on February 5, 1996. I was there in the delivery room, watching the magical process, my weak knees wobbling. It was the most complete day of my life. When I held my daughter, what I wanted with all my being was to marry Sonia, to become a family.

In the aftermath of my conversation with Mr. Sepulveda, our relationship fell apart. It occurred to me suddenly that there might be something wrong with me, or something imperfect in my love. Of course, both statements were true. I got drunk with some friends and they counseled me to forget her. I revised history: no longer frightened to my core of marriage and fatherhood, I became in my mind a jilted man who wanted to take responsibility for his child, a man cruelly rebuffed without cause. I told everyone in earshot I wanted to marry her, safe in the knowledge that it was an impossibility. And in the space of a few months I called every woman who had ever smiled at me. I took these women dancing and bought them drinks, spent lavishly on their entertainment, and slept with as many as would have me.

It was an accomplishment just to be allowed in the delivery room. A negotiation. Sonia didn't want to see me. I insisted that I had rights and she relented. Once there, I was despondent and inspired, hopeful and depressed, aware of the pain I had caused Sonia. I saw Mayra's little legs and little arms and the slick newness of her tiny face. Her hazel eyes were the same color as her mother's, and the two of them were in that moment my religion. I found myself wanting to cry at the beauty of her tiny body, her unblemished personhood. And at what I had done. My selfish crimes seemed an insurmountable obstacle if I were ever to be her father.

Sonia and Mayra were waiting for me on the step of the hostel when I walked up. It had been a week or so since I last saw them, long enough for my appearance to be an event. My little girl squirmed out from her mother's embrace, took one awkward step toward me and stood in my way. She had her arms crossed and her face frozen in a grimace. What theater! Her black bangs tickled her forehead. I knelt before her and offered her my cheek for a kiss.

"Do you know today is my birthday?" she asked gravely.

I looked up and caught Sonia smiling. I asked her in a tremulous voice if this was true.

"I'm afraid so."

"Well," I said, reaching into the inside pocket of my suit jacket, "then I'm glad I didn't give this away."

Mayra's eyes opened wide with wonder. It was a small, thin package, the makeup kit. The wrapping paper was red and green, a festive Christmas pattern that looked out of place in February. Mayra didn't seem to mind.

"Mayra honey," Sonia said, "why don't we go upstairs and open it."

It was too late. It would be opened right there, on the sidewalk between the step and the street. She was already tearing into the paper, using her little hands and her teeth and all of her urgent enthusiasm.

Sonia stood from the step and gave me a kiss, slipping her right arm under my jacket and around my back. She whispered a question in my ear, why I was late, and I mumbled a response about telling her later. She said she had something to tell me too, then she bit my earlobe softly.

The package, once opened, left Mayra a bit befuddled. It was a simple gift really, with two lipsticks, a small hairbrush, and some powders and blushes that I thought might be fun for my little girl to play with. She was stuck on the box. "Is she old enough for this?" I asked.

Sonia frowned and knelt down to take a closer look.

"What is it?" Mayra asked.

"It'll make you even more beautiful than you already are," I said.

"Lipstick!" Mayra exclaimed. She had pried it free, twisted the bottom until it was fully extended, standing in a shiny red salute.

"You couldn't have gotten her a book?" Sonia asked.

"I want her to like me."

She smirked. "What do you say, Mayra, baby?"

"Thank you, Papi," my daughter purred, and all the day's small troubles and all the grander ones seemed distant and unimportant.

"Next year Daddy's going to get you a book," I said.

Mayra stuck her tongue out. I scooped her into my arms.

There was a movie to see and ice cream to have and balloons and conversation and strolling and hugs. For the first time in Mayra's short life, I let Sonia pay. When I pulled out the fifteen soles I had, she wouldn't take them. We took a cab to Miraflores and walked along the boardwalk, high above the sea. The summer sun slipped toward dusk in lurid red streaks. We stopped at the park to watch the hang gliders, dozens of them floating high above the city's coastline.

Mayra had never seen them before. She asked if they were giant birds.

I said they were, but Sonia shook her head. Poor Mayra looked at the both of us, bewildered.

"What *are* they then, babe?" I asked Sonia.

"Not giant birds," she said, backtracking. "No, no. Enormous birds."

"Is that bigger than giant?" Mayra asked.

I reassured her it was, and she seemed pleased.

I put Mayra on my shoulders so she could have a better look. She squinted against the dying sun, pointing at them as they swept in slow motion, left and right above the horizon. I took Sonia's hand in mine, and she gave it to me easily. Enough time has passed, I thought. Tonight she might finally say yes.

I have proposed in her parents' home. In a fine restaurant, after wine and dinner served by waiters with European accents. At the zoo, two years ago, with balloons and a trumpet I'd borrowed from a friend. And on Mayra's fourth birthday, in the naked intimacy of Sonia's bedroom. Last year, like every year, she told me she loved me but wasn't sure that was enough. I told her it was enough for me, that I loved her. It's not that I haven't thought of giving up; it's that I don't know how.

A few months after Mayra was born, Sonia traveled to the States to learn English. Her family wanted to get her away from me, from the stress. For half a year I visited my daughter three times a week, suffered through awkward silences with the Sepulvedas, who didn't know whether to hate me or applaud my persistence. I sat on their sofa, under the dour gaze of Mrs. Sepulveda, rocking little Mayra in my arms. At night I created scenarios that ranged from the tragic to the blessed: Sonia in the States, meeting a man who swept her off her feet. A tall, white man. A rich man. A man more handsome and more intelligent than myself. Kinder certainly. A better father. These were my nightmares when I thought I had lost her. But I let myself dream as well: Sonia returning, chastened by what she had seen there, overwhelmed by the depravity her father had described, forgiving, wanting a fresh start.

Back when I worked for my uncle, we made a delivery once in San Juan de Lurigancho. I left the back door of the van unlocked. We were only inside a few minutes, but when we came out, it was open, and a few scraggly dressed kids were running off with boxes of foundation and perfumed lotions and soaps. We started to chase after them, when the owner said she recognized the thieves. Come back later, she said. I'll straighten this out. We made a few more deliveries, came back a couple hours later, and followed the woman to the first child's home. It was humble, the door made of wooden slats so poorly constructed you could stick your fingers through the yawning gaps. A small woman let us in, listened with her hands behind her back as we explained what had happened. The home smelled of boiled vegetables and mud. The sheepish child appeared when he was called, twelve at most and barefoot. My uncle spoke. The boy curled his toes into the dirt floor and rocked back on his heels. His mother apologized profusely. Then the boy left and reappeared with a box of fingernail polishes. My uncle noted there was one missing.

"I used it," his mother said. "It was a gift." She held her colored nails out for us to see.

Her nails were painted a deep, earthy red. "It looks very nice," I told her.

I remember telling Sonia this story, years ago. It was a late morning in bed and she sat on top of me, drawing her name on my chest and stomach with a blue ballpoint pen. When she pressed hard into my skin, it tickled.

When I got to this point in the story, she looked up. "What did you do?" she asked. Her hair fell in my face.

The truth is my uncle took the nail polish. He resealed it and we sold it. He apologized to the woman and he felt terrible, but he did it. Money was tight.

"We let her keep it," I said. I'm not sure why I lied. It just seemed so terrible.

Sonia went back to her work, her tongue poking out, applying another baroque *S* to my body. I tried to peek over my chin to see.

"What?" I asked.

"I mean, weren't you broke? Wasn't your family broke?"

"You would have taken it from her?"

"It wasn't nail polish she needed."

"It was a start!"

"Oh, Miguel," Sonia said and kissed my stomach. "First take care of your own, babe. That's what I've always been told."

The woman didn't protest. She thanked us politely for not going to the police. I exchanged glances with the boy, knowing he wouldn't be punished. He knew it too. He hadn't done anything wrong. He was sure of it.

I lay there, felt the nib of the ballpoint pen tracing letters on my skin. I closed my eyes and Sonia laughed exquisitely. "I'm done," she announced. "You can look now."

When I opened my eyes, she pulled off her shirt in one quick move. It amazed me. Her breasts were small and round. She handed me the pen. "Now it's your turn," she said, smiling. She closed her eyes and waited. "Hurry!"

We were in the cab riding home when she told me Mayra had received another gift for her birthday, that it had come in the mail and that it was postmarked from the United States. There was a heaviness in her voice that surprised me.

"Really?" I asked. It was late and I felt suddenly tired. "From your uncle?"

She shook her head. From an American. A travel writer who had written a review. He had stayed awhile in Lima. Apparently I'd met him. Didn't I remember? Sure. The tall man, the white man, the rich man of my nightmares.

"I didn't realize you were staying in touch," I said. "That's nice."

The city was dark, our daughter asleep between the two of us.

"He wants me to come visit him. He said he can help us get the visa."

"Us?" I asked.

"Me and Mayra."

I felt myself nod and was aware that my daughter's tiny feet lay across my lap. I had the impulse to hold her, to turn her so that her cheek rested against my chest.

"Are you going to go?"

"He's paying for the tickets."

"Are you going to stay?" I asked.

"I don't know."

The cab moved swiftly along the dimly lit streets. Along Tacna, thickets of people waited for buses that would carry them home, crowds thronged around the entrances to underground clubs. Techno music attacked our silence. We were almost there, to the New Lima. I'd told her already about my run-in with the law, self-consciously omitting details until the whole episode sounded like fragments of surrealist poetry. I'd spoken of my impending financial ruin and again felt the humiliating rush of blood to my face. We'd lapsed into silence. She knew all of my secrets and now I knew hers. She was leaving me for *Los Uniteds*, for its mighty economy, its fertile ground where dollars grow wild. He wouldn't be taking her to *Nueva Jersey*, I assumed, but somewhere with verdant lawns and dustless houses, a place where newness hung in the air like perfume. Why wouldn't she go? And if she left, why would she return?

"Do you love him?" I asked.

She nodded. "You can love more than one person at a time," she said.

We were silent until the hostel. There we put Mayra to bed, the sweet smallness of her, innocent of our machinations and our troubles. At what age would she begin to understand? How many years did I have left before she would recognize me for the failure I was? How many more before she forgot me?

Sonia and I drifted back into the drab front lobby. Above the counter was the starred review in a cheap wooden frame. I tapped the glass with my knuckle, wanting to shatter it. "Is this it?" I asked.

The three couches were set at right angles to one another. She collapsed into the one by the far wall. There was a high window above it and a wan yellow light fell into the lobby. She didn't answer me.

I felt fidgety. I couldn't sit or stand. I paced in front of the counter. I had scarcely eaten all day and felt suddenly light-headed. "What's his name?" I asked.

"It doesn't matter."

"Where does he live?"

"Nowhere."

"Is he rich?"

"He isn't rich."

"Do you miss him? Is he blond? Do you speak English with him? Does he e-mail you, call you, send you pictures?"

"Stop," she said.

I was drunk with questions, walking tight circles in front of her.

Sonia let out a sigh. "This isn't exactly how I imagined my life."

In this city, there is nothing more useless than imagining a life. Tomorrow is as unknowable as next year, and there is nothing solid to grab hold of. There is no work. There is nothing I could have promised her in that moment that wouldn't have been built on imagination. Or worse, on luck.

"What do you expect me to do?" she asked, watching me through the long seconds of my silence. "What would you do?"

"I don't know," I said finally.

"You'd do what's best for her."

I slumped in the sofa to her right and closed my eyes tightly. My ears were ringing. "So it's just for her," I said through gritted teeth. "And poor little you has to leave and move to Gringoland."

"I don't want to fight."

"Just say what's on your mind."

She sucked her teeth. "You remind me of every mistake I've ever made."

"That's funny. Because you remind me of our daughter."

"Not her," she said. "I wasn't talking about her."

"Of course you weren't. I get it. You want new mistakes."

"Why not?" She stood up, suddenly angry. There was heat in her voice. "Let me guess," she said. "You have the ring in your pocket. You want to get down on one knee and read me a love poem and you want me to cry and you want me to want you. But I'll say no because I'm the only one who thinks between the two of us, and so you'll disappear for a month to lick your wounds and I'll have to hear from Mayra that her daddy picked her up from kindergarten, that he brought her a present."

I was sweating. "What about us?" I asked.

She stared at me for a moment, disbelieving. I thought so many things between us had been forgiven. "Why didn't you fight for me?" she said.

I started to answer—that I was, that I had been for five years—but she cut me off. "Not now—then."

It felt terrible to have nothing to say.

"I never wanted to *have* to get married. I wanted to *want* to get married."

"Do you *want* to marry this guy?"

"He hasn't asked me yet," she said. "But he will."

It was nearly midnight. The soft sounds of traffic drifted in through the window. I needed to think. I pulled out my fifteen soles and asked her for a room on the empty fourth floor with a view and a balcony. Sonia looked at me perplexed.

"This is a hostel, isn't it?" I said. "Are Peruvians not allowed to stay here?"

In the pale light I could see her glaring at me.

"I'm sorry."

"Fifteen's not enough."

"I'm good for it."

Sonia stood and walked around the counter. She ran her finger along the keys, pulling one off its hook and handing it to me. "You know the way up."

I asked her to wait.

I went to the back room and fumbled in the dark until my eyes adjusted. Mayra was sleeping. I picked her up, careful not to wake her. She molded her sleep to my embrace with barely a murmur. I stepped out into the light and saw Sonia sitting on the counter, her legs swinging against the wood. She looked so young.

"I love you, Miguel," she said. "But marrying you would be like giving up."

She handed me the key and kissed me good night.

I watched Mayra breathe for a while and dozed off. I awoke to Sonia moving through the shadows of the room and into bed. Our daughter slept between us, the only honest person in her family.

I drifted into sleep again and dreamed, this time for real, such saturated, overblown dreams that when I woke up just after dawn the whole of the previous day seemed perversely dreamlike too. Were they leaving? Were they already gone?

Sonia was asleep on her side, facing me, with an arm over Mayra.

After a while I got out of bed and pulled back the curtains to find that daybreak had exploded over Lima again. I was filled with inexplicable energy, though I hadn't slept much, and an optimism that bordered on delusion. The emptiness in my stomach was gone. They wouldn't leave, I thought. They couldn't.

Sonia groaned and covered her eyes. Mayra grumbled and turned over. "Papi!" she complained.

"Ladies and gentlemen!" I said grandly, with a sweep of my arms. "The sunrise!"

Sonia rolled over into her pillow, muffling a tiny laugh, and then popped up. She smiled weakly at me, then fell into a deep full-body yawn, catlike, that ended with her outstretched toes poking out from beneath the sheet. "Wake up, honey," she said to Mayra. Then to me, "Good morning."

I let the sun pour in through the window, lighting her smile. Then Mayra was awake and sitting up in bed. "Daddy," she called out, pointing at my belly. "You're fat!"

"Mayra!" Sonia said. "Don't be rude!"

But it seemed so funny to me. I laughed. I'm not fat; it's just that I'm not young anymore. I grabbed my belly and pretended for a moment my navel was a bullet hole, that I was mortally wounded. I crumpled to the ground, "Oh, Mayra," I called out.

My daughter crawled over to the edge of the bed and hung there, looking me in the eyes as I lay on the floor. Her black hair stood up in places, a wild mane of tangles. She broke into a wide, goofy smile and I closed my eyes.

Imagine, as I did then, time in the form of a narrowing tunnel, pulling your loved ones farther and still farther from you. Distances expanding relentlessly, life reduced to memories of people who have gone away. Imagine the odd and terrible silences, the emptied spaces. Imagine withering in this place alone. See your daughter in a faraway northern nation, with its cold winds and heavy rains, struggling to distinguish you from a slew of blurred sights and sounds and smells. Imagine memory's illogic has buried you behind the noise of this city's traffic or the scent of the New Lima's musty hallways—imagine: *people and things I can barely recall, a report by Mayra Solis* and somewhere in that forlorn text: her father! Imagine she forgets her Spanish, and all her fears and hopes and loves and dreams are trapped, lost in a vault of foreign sounds.

Sonia said something, and then I could hear the voice of my daughter, but my thoughts were elsewhere, or else they were so precisely there they were underground, boring holes in the earth beneath the city, or floating just above it, tying ribbons to the tallest trees. I stood up slowly. I think Sonia must have recognized the flight I was on because she fell silent. Squinting against the light, she watched me and I watched her.

"What?" she asked.

I am a man of traditions, and because I am that man, I bent down on one knee, again, one final time. Sunlight gathered in the room, a breeze circled and blew the curtains apart. Sonia shook her head—no, no—but I kept on. My daughter had clambered back on the bed and sat, her legs underneath her, watching us as if it were theater. And there were no trumpets or violins or sounds at all. Only quiet. I took the ring from the inside of my jacket. "Sonia," I said, and played my last card, and so, regret nothing.

a strong dead man

Rafael's father started to die in March. By summer, it was nearly complete. It came upon him all at once, a summer storm brewed from a cloudless sky, and rendered him—in quick and cold fashion—a ghost, a negative image, weak and formless, a fourth cup from a single bag of tea. Rafael watched in muted horror as a succession of strokes reduced his father ever further. Nearly dust by the end. He learned that life makes us older frantically, that time does not always pass in an even cadence, but sometimes all at once: that we can age—months, years, decades—in a single day, even a single hour.

For Rafael, that hour came on a Sunday in June, the day of his father's third stroke, just at the end of the school year. He was sixteen. Outside, music swept off Dykman Avenue. A throaty bass from each passing car drifted into his family's third-floor apartment. Aunts and uncles and cousins had arrived, making all the sounds of grieving: whimpering, crying, whispering, laughing so as not to cry. The curtains were pulled, but through the thin fabric Rafael could make out the brick wall just beyond the window. There was another apartment, another life just beyond that. The room where he sat was dark and hot.

Suitcases lay open. The last stroke had come that morning as they were planning to travel home to Santo Domingo. Rafael felt the skin of his thighs sticking to the plastic covers of the sofa cushions. In the next room, his mother slept at the foot of her bed, an unthinking, drugged sleep. His aunts spoke about him and his father as if Rafael could not hear.

"Poor thing. They took him away almost dead. He couldn't recognize his own wife."

"Did the boy see it?"

"He was here the whole time. He hasn't said a word since."

He hadn't. Rafael had begun to understand that life bends you, forms you, creates the spaces you fill without hope or interest in the particulars of your plans. He had none. His mother got a sleeping pill after she cried and cried, her eyes and face nearly bursting with red, all tears and sweat, but Rafael was quiet and said nothing and so he got nothing and was not spoken to. This is it, he thought. Life is bending me. His aunt Aida paced nervously in the small room. "*Dios mío*, it's hot," she said. He didn't answer. She pulled back the curtain, but no light came in.

Whispers. A door. His cousin had come. From the hallway, a voice.

"What happened?" Mario called. The heels of his dress shoes rapped against the wooden floor.

Aida, his mother, hugged her son tightly and told him, "A stroke, *papito*. They took your uncle to the hospital . . ." She couldn't finish. Her breath seemed to run out on her and she was left only with sobs. Mario consoled his mother while she cried. Rafael could tell that Mario's eyes hadn't yet adjusted to the peculiar twilight of the apartment; his cousin squinted behind metal frames. I'm here, Rafael thought, on the couch. Can you see me?

From the kitchen, another aunt appeared with a plate of white rice and *habichuelas*. "Eat, Mario," she said. Steam rose from the warm plate, but Mario shook his head. Aida pulled away, wiped her eyes with a pink paper napkin.

"And Rafael?" Mario asked. His voice was concerned, but calm. "How is he?" He turned to face his cousin, looking blankly at the wall beyond the window. "Are you all right?"

Rafael shrugged. Mario's question was warbled and scratchy, like a voice from behind glass. Mario turned back to his mother. "I'll take him. He should get out of the house. I'll talk to him." Aida sighed. The room was full of silences. Mario motioned to Rafael, and he rose quietly. They walked down the long hallway, closing the door softly behind them.

They wandered west on Dykman to the river, to the park where Rafael had seen his only dead body. This was years before, seventh grade, twelve years old and loud, in a pack of friends six deep. They had stared off the pier at 208th Street, three in the afternoon, three-thirty, the bridge to the south, an escape, to the north, the river, green and wide and beautiful. They had gazed across the Hudson, at the wooded bluffs of Jersey, spotted with white mansions peering out among the trees. "Damn, who lives there?" Patrick Ewing, they decided, or someone else rich and famous and young.

Amir saw it first, drifting against the rocks beneath the pier. "Oh shit! Look at that shit!" he yelled. They got down on their knees to see. Rafael, Jaime, Carl, Javier, Eric, and Amir. None would admit they were afraid. Carl lived in Grant down on 125th, but he went to school up in Dykman because his mother worked at the hospital. "He looks like a Spanish nigga," Carl said.

The body's skin was brown, a shade or two lighter than the river itself.

The body wore only a pair of black shorts.

The body's back was rippled with muscles. Rafael thought to himself, That's a strong dead man, and the idea made him laugh, so he said it aloud. "That's a strong dead man."

"Well, *somebody* must've been stronger."

Amir was the funny one. They laughed, and Rafael felt good. He was new to the school and made friends only by accident: on the walk home, by lockers that faced each other, at desks that sat side by side. Friends had never been easy.

"He's got a damn plastic bag stuck on his foot."

"That's fucked up."

"That shit ain't right."

They stayed at the pier, talking, until the conversation moved away from the body, and soon they were all seated, their legs dangling off the edge. They remembered him only when the Circle Line passed, gliding down the river, a boat full of tourists waving and taking pictures. "You think they can see him?" Rafael asked. His first instinct was to run.

"Naw, they're too far. There's no way," Amir said.

Then Javier waved back because Javier was like that and Carl and Amir laughed at him and called him a pussy. "With my arm, I could hit that boat, no doubt," Carl bragged, and Rafael smiled, though he didn't believe him. Beneath them, the body came and went against the shore. They glared at the Circle Line and none of them knew why they hated that boat so much.

Mario and Rafael didn't stop at the pier. Instead, they found a place to sit at the fields, letting their eyes wander as the games unfolded before them. The day was bright and clear, the park brimming. A man carried a wooden board pegged with colorful balloons. A Chinese couple laid out bootleg videos on a blanket spread on the grass. So many bikes whizzed by that the ground itself seemed to move—a giant conveyer belt this island—and the only ones still were Mario and Rafael. They sat in the sun between fields, where they could watch two games at once. Mario had bought them both sodas, and the games slid by as they sipped from straws, their plastic bottles pimpled with condensation. Rafael was glad to be outdoors.

He could tell how tired his cousin was. His slacks and dress shoes looked out of place, he had unbuttoned and untucked his shirt. Mario's hair was black and unruly and should have been cut weeks ago. Everyone was always saying that he put in too many hours—he'd come from work that very day. But to Rafael it seemed exciting to have tasks to complete and people who depended on you. Mario had gone to college and worked in a bank now, something with computers. He called them systems. He was ten years older than Rafael.

For a long while they said nothing and were comfortable, the bright day being so far and so different from where they had come. Then, slowly, they were talking, Rafael surprised that they could speak of something else. They wagered as to who would get on base. Mario had the science. "You size up the hitter," he said, "by taking in the complete picture. Don't be fooled by his physique."

"The whole package?"

"Fat don't mean he can't run and skinny don't mean he can't hit. Look for confidence. The way he carries himself, even between pitches."

They eyed a hitter as he came to the plate. His uniform hung off him, a little too big, enough to highlight the thin arms and puny legs that carried him. He was fidgety, adjusting and readjusting his cap. The pitcher waited. "He's gonna strike out," Rafael said. "He's nervous."

The batter kicked his left cleat up against the barrel of the bat; a tiny cloud of dust materialized and then vanished. Mario nodded.

The first pitch came in high, but he chased it, nearly falling over in the process. There were some snickers from the opposing team. The hitter took his time, a few mock swings, before getting back to the plate. He looked lost already. The next pitch sailed by him, a called strike. 0–2. Mario nudged his cousin. "Good call. He's done." Rafael smiled. The hitter called time and, taking off his cap, looked sheepishly toward the dugout. Half his guys were already getting their gloves on. None of them would meet his gaze. The pitcher smelled blood. The hitter stepped back in, got in his stance. The pitch was a good one, but the swing was all wrong, defensive, tenuous. He popped the ball high toward first. He didn't even run.

"Damn. Good call," Mario repeated.

They watched a few more, and some surprised them. A little rail of a man slapped a double, driving in a run. An overmatched pitcher got a slugger to ground out. Before long, Rafael found himself rooting for the batter, even though he had been a pitcher in Little League. He saw no contradiction in switching allegiances when the teams switched sides. Rafael loved the way a pitcher's face dropped at the crack of the bat or the way he followed the ball's long flight into left field with a look of resignation. "Do it!" Rafael shouted. "Run, run!" he yelled. "Beat the throw! Slide!"

After a while the sun got too strong, and they walked past the soccer game to the next set of diamonds where there was shade. It seemed like the whole world was in the park, everyone pitting themselves and their skills against each other. Rafael was not an athlete, hadn't thrived in competition. His Little League glove now collected dust in a corner of the room he shared with his sister. It came back to him, though, the smell of it, the slant of the shadows on the field, the simple rules he had once played by. He never hated his opponents, could never convince himself he did, and had wondered on the mound, holding the ball in his sweaty palm, if the batters hated him. Rafael rattled easily, took each hit personally. A fielding error turned his stomach to knots—are they sabotaging me? my own teammates?—and by the eighth grade he had lost interest in playing. He threw weakly, or thought he did, but missed that feeling of pure joy when, after throwing hard and fast for hours and hours, his arm became jelly, throbbing and nearly glowing. There was something wonderful there: every tendon stretched, a vague tingling. Is that what it feels like, Rafael thought, what my father felt? After the first stroke in March, Rafael had sat with him, watched his father and the confused way in which he observed his own limbs. "I'll be okay," his father had said, but he had no movement in his left side. His eyes darted from his son to his own useless arm and back again. "What's going to happen?" Rafael had asked.

"I'm getting better. This is just a small thing," his father said. He forced a smile, and Rafael believed him.

Mario and Rafael hung on the fence by the northernmost field and watched a pitcher bully his way through a couple of innings. He threw like a monster, strictly heat. Fastballs from an abbreviated windup, tight with scarcely a kick of the leg. Boom against the catcher's leather. Hitter after hitter watched pitches go by, the ball slapped solidly against the mitt. His teammates cheered him on. Nobody could get around on his fastball, and the smugness of him was too much. He was killing them. He wore a little mustache that he stroked between pitches, and smiled cruelly when a ball went foul, as if he was surprised the batter had even made contact. Rafael bristled at his arrogance. He wanted to see him hit, could imagine it: a drive up the middle, driven hard to the thighs, to the stomach, to the chest. Why not?

Mario liked him. "This kid can throw," he said.

"He's a dick."

"He's good, Rafael. That's it."

Rafael was aware that they had been at the park and out of the house for over an hour now and had not shared a single word about why they were there. It was better this way. He felt no particular need to speak of it, to speak of his father. It was happening. He was at the hospital, or perhaps they had brought him home by now. Or perhaps he would never leave the hospital alive. He thought of his mother, asleep, calm for the first time in weeks.

She had no interest in ever waking up.

"I could tell you a story, Rafa, but I'm not sure you'd even believe me," Mario said, breaking the silence. He took off his dress shirt, draping it over his head. "It's too bizarre, almost unbelievable." Rafael didn't answer him, but only looked on. Mario sighed.

"Whatever . . . I was ten. We lived on 181st. I liked to ride my bike all over the place, I mean all over. Down to 116th, to Riverside, all around Dykman. Me and some kids rode all the way to Yankee Stadium a couple of times. I mean, we just loved to go places, see things. My moms couldn't really keep an eye on me, she was working and all, so I was sort of left to mind myself. I did all right, not great but all right. We were good kids. Then one day, I'm out and I'm alone and I'm riding by myself, and I swear to God, I'm there just cruising down the sidewalk, and there's a shot, and before I have time to look up—you won't believe this—this body has landed on me. Fell from the second floor, third floor—what do I know? A man. Straight knocked me off my bike. I swear to God! A fucking body. Straight knocked me over. I didn't even look at him. I didn't even breathe. I got back on my bike and rode and rode and rode, don't know how I got home, but I did. Then I put that bike away and started playing video games, kid. Full-time. I mean, I got fat. You couldn't get me out of the house, I was so fucking scared. I mean months. I watched TV and played video games and never got on that bike again."

Mario sighed, laughing, shaking his head. Rafael just stared. It was the most ridiculous thing he'd ever heard. "You ever told anybody?" he asked.

"Naw. Not my moms, not a soul. No one would have believed me. I don't know why I just told you. . . ," Mario stammered, "but I did. And you can do what you want with it. Fuck it, forget it."

Rafael shook his head. "Can't forget that, cousin."

He thought of the body he had seen, not even a hundred yards from where they sat. Rafael had never told anyone either. He thought of the plastic bag clinging to the man's foot and was suddenly ashamed. His mind curved down a spiral of dark thoughts, but he turned away, stopping that chain of memories cold. Instead, he smacked Mario playfully. "You look like a fucking habibi with that shirt on your head!" Mario laughed his big laugh and Rafael smiled, eyes closed against the sun.

All dead men don't fall from the sky. They don't all float down the Hudson and come to rest against smooth moss-covered rocks at the water's edge. Some of them are your fathers, your uncles. Some of them lose the battle slowly. Some die hating the world. Rafael wondered what his father was thinking or if he was at all anymore. Beyond the trees, there was shimmer: a glaze of hazy sunlight hung over the water.

They sat in silence a while, submerged in the sounds of the park. The game ended and another began. It was a joke, all of it. Nameless, faceless dead. Bodies raining down on city sidewalks, throwing children off bicycles. They'd been gone for hours now. The breeze picked up plastic bags and candy wrappers and carried them off to the river. From there they would ride to the ocean. It was time to head back. There were still hours of light left, but in Rafael's apartment it would be dusk. In Rafael's apartment they would be waiting for news and his mother would still be asleep. He would come home and they would tell him nothing. And this would go on for two more days before they would tell him the only thing he didn't want to hear. Rafael saw his father then, extinguished, his skin sallow and ashen, his arms at his side. They buried him. A week later, the family was home again, under an empty Caribbean sun, receiving condolences from people with faces and names Rafael didn't recognize. The Spanish they spoke slipped off their tongues too fast, and he couldn't be sure of what he heard and what he misunderstood. It was like a dream. On the tenth day, his mother's sleeping pills ran out and he fell asleep to the muffled sound of her sobbing. He thought of his father. Every minute of every hour, he thought of his father, and of Mario and the park. He thought of the water lapping over the dead man's body, and the plastic bag around his foot. He thought of bodies falling from the skies. He wished he had been there to see the body fall. He wished he could have been there to catch him. To hold him up. To look him in the face and say, "Live! Live! Live!

acknowledgments

I owe many people for many gifts. It's a bit self-indulgent to try to thank them all, but I'll give it a shot. My teachers, who have given generously of their time and wisdom: Paul McAdam, Mark Slouka, Colin Harrison, Ethan Canin, Chris Offutt, Edward Carey, Elizabeth McCracken, and ZZ Packer. Alan Ziegler and Leslie Woodward have been friends and supporters for many years. Kathleen McDermott has always looked out for me. Frank Conroy challenged and encouraged me to work harder; for this I am in his debt.

I rely on good friends for inspiration and, often, for sanity: Antonio Garcia, Agustin Vecino, Maggie Berryman, Laura Rysman, Danny Rudder, Andre Morales, Zea Malawa, Adrienne Brown, Josh Seidenfeld, Pascual Mejia, Stacey White, Scott Wolven, Claudia Manley, Clay Colvin, Caroline Wingo, Neil Roy, Wayne Yeh, John Green, Emmett Cloud, Shazi Visram, and Sean Titone—all beautiful people with big hearts. Sonia Gulati, with love. Carlos Aguasaco, *mi compa.* Mario Michelena, *mi primo, mi colega.* Jai Chun, wherever you are. The Class of 2003 at Bread and Roses Integrated Arts High School in New York, for putting up with a first-year teacher. To Olivia Armenta, for innumerable gifts.

In Lima, the Aronés family looked after me while I lived in San Juan de Lurigancho. All of my friends from AAHH 10 de Octubre and AAHH Jose Carlos Mariátegui, especially Vico Vargas Sulca, Jhon Lenon Mariño Yupanqui, Geral Huaripata Vasquez, Cesar Ortiz, Jorge "Koky" Ramos, and Roller Li Alzamora. The Diaz Tena family from Cruz de Motupe, especially Carmela. Everyone involved with the Defensores de La Paz Project, especially Carla Rimac, Jenny Uribe, and Olenka Ochoa from Incafam. The folks from Fulbright in Lima were great, always helpful and supportive, especially Migza and Marcela. Carlos Villacorta, for his friendship and his poetry. Pepe Alvarez, Felipe Leon—*hermano*! Lucy Naldos, Betsy Zapata, Mauricio Delfin—these are friends I can count on.

My family: the Alarcón clan, from Lima to Arequipa to La Paz; the Solis Diaspora, from Lima to Sweden to New York to Belgium. Claudy is my friend and confidante. I couldn't have written this book or any book without the folks I met at Iowa: writers, poets, artists, and all-around wonderful people—too many to name. A few people deserve special mention for being great friends and great readers: Dave Sarno, Lila "Stealthy" Byock, Vinnie Wilhelm, Mark Lafferty, Kerrie Kvashay-Boyle, Sam Shaw, Grace Lee, and Mika Tanner.

Thanks also to Guillermo Martinez, Hugo Chaparro, Alejandra Costamagna, and Cristian Gomez for their advice and encouragement. Connie Brothers, Deb West, and Jan Zenisek have made my life easier. Thanks to the Foxhead, for existing, to Prairie Lights, to the Wobblies, for a winning season and a shot at glory. Ricardo Gutierrez, for the book recommendations. Nicholas Pearson, for his insight. Susan and Linda at

Glimmer Train, for buying my first story. Julio Villanueva Chang from Etiqueta Negra. Leelila Strogov at Swink. Deborah Treisman, for the education and the opportunity.

An extra-special big dawg thank-you to my comrade in the struggle, Eric Simonoff, who made it happen, and my editor, Alison Callahan, for her guidance and confidence. Thanks also to René Alegria, mi patrón at Rayo and a good friend.

Finally, my parents, Renato and Chela, and my sisters, Patricia and Sylvia, to whom I've dedicated this book. I owe them everything. To my newest family: Pat, Marcela, and Lucia.

About the author

About the book

Read on

Insights,
Interviews
& More . . .

About the author

Meet Daniel Alarcón

© 2005 by Olivia Armenta

DANIEL ALARCÓN, the son of two physicians, was born in Lima, Peru. He moved (at age three) to Birmingham, Alabama, in 1980. There he enjoyed a "very pleasant" childhood. "It was," he says, "a rather average suburban middle-class American upbringing in the South—except we spoke Spanish at home."

He returned to Peru almost annually. "Our family back there was always very supportive of us," he says.

His earliest memory of reading stretches back to first grade. "You could order little kid books from the Scholastic Book Club," he says. "I went home and asked to order a book, and my mom said no because I couldn't yet read English. I really redoubled my efforts at reading after that."

"He first worked as a grocery bagger for Food World."

He first worked as a grocery bagger for Food World. ("Coincidentally," he notes, "my family's first residence in Alabama was in an apartment just above the same grocery store.")

Another job found him delivering food for "something called Takeout Taxi." His coworkers included a foursome with emphatically comic and counterproductive forenames. "The highlight was that there were four guys named Vladimir working with us," he says. "It was all run on walkie-talkies, so if all four of them were working the same night they were given ridiculous names to distinguish them: Vladimir, Vlady, Vlad 1, and Vlad 2. At age sixteen I found this infinitely amusing. I drove all over suburban Birmingham and saw a lot of very unhappy people eating overpriced food alone."

He attended college at Columbia University. The anthropology major placed himself at the center of student protests during his freshman year. Agitating for the addition of more ethnic studies courses, he participated in major demonstrations within Low Library and other facilities. On the day following the library protest he joined an outdoor rally on the steps of the main administrative building. It was here, on these steps, that he suffered an ignoble but strangely beneficial fate. "This was the spring of 1996," he says. "One of the more visible people in the protests was making a speech in front of a large crowd that had gathered, and I was holding the megaphone for him when a bird shat on me—right on top of my head. I passed the megaphone off to someone else and went to my dorm room to take a shower. When I came back a half hour later, all my friends had been arrested."

His regrettable association with birds extends well beyond the wild groves of academe. Indeed, it suggests a bizarre ▶

"'One of the more visible people in the protests was making a speech in front of a large crowd that had gathered, and I was holding the megaphone for him when a bird shat on me—right on top of my head.'"

Meet Daniel Alarcón ***(continued)***

chronicle best examined by an ornithologist or (at any rate) a martyrologist. "Birds have shat on me more than ten times in my life," he says, "including four times in the past twelve months—three times in one very odd week in January."

He worked in a copy shop for three years during college. Upon graduation he worked as a counselor for one year at a housing project in East Harlem, then taught tenth-grade English for one year at a public school in Central Harlem.

He returned to Peru in 2001 as a Fulbright Scholar and taught photography in San Juan de Lurigancho, a marginal district of northeastern Lima. His extended visit satisfied a personal forecast: "When I was fifteen, my parents and I were watching a CNN report about a slum in Lima," he says, "and I told my mom that one day I was going to live in a slum like that. She laughed and laughed and laughed. . . ."

" 'When I was fifteen, my parents and I were watching a CNN report about a slum in Lima," he says, "and I told my mom that one day I was going to live in a slum like that. She laughed and laughed and laughed.' "

He earned a Master of Fine Arts degree from the Iowa Writers' Workshop.

He has recently enjoyed books by David Bezmozgis *(Natasha: And Other Stories)*, Sukhetu Mehta *(Maximum City: Bombay Lost and Found)*, and Roberto Bolaño *(La Pista de Hielo)*.

His literary routine does not include weekends ("I don't believe in overworking") and makes canny use of stimulants ("I drink coffee, but never more than two cups a day—one in the morning, one in mid-afternoon").

Among his extraliterary enthusiasms are

soccer, dice, the Oakland A's, and "trying to become a decent salsa dancer."

His fiction has appeared in many magazines, including *The New Yorker, Harper's,* and *Virginia Quarterly Review,* and has been anthologized in *Best American Non-Required Reading* (2004 and 2005). His nonfiction has appeared in *Salon* and *Eyeshot*. He is associate editor of the Lima-based magazine *Etiqueta Negra*. The recipient of a 2004 Whiting Writers' Award, he lives in Oakland, California, where (as Distinguished Visiting Writer at Mills College) he teaches fiction.

He has a cat named Mecha, which in Peruvian slang means "to fight." ("She's very feisty. I have the scratches to prove it.")

He is writing a novel called *Lost City Radio.*

About the book

A Slum, a Boy Named Lennon, Some Dancing in the Street—Peru Revisited

My family left Lima in 1980 (when I was three years old) to live in the United States. We sent letters and audio diaries to our cousins back home and visited quite a bit until 1989, when the war got bad. Then, somehow, six years passed between visits. I went off to school in New York and another four years passed.

I was twenty-four when I returned to live for a while in Peru. I wasn't deliberately researching a book—but of course that's what ended up happening. The city where I was born had nearly doubled in size to a population of over eight million. The war was over, and a decade of economic liberalism had thrown the country—for good or ill—headfirst into the global system. I'm not sure exactly what I was expecting upon my return, but I was completely unprepared for the depth of the changes—social, cultural, and economic—reshaping Lima.

“I'm not sure exactly what I was expecting upon my return, but I was completely unprepared for the depth of the changes reshaping Lima.”

I rented a room in San Juan de Lurigancho and set up a project there to teach photography. San Juan is a dusty and poor district rising northeast of Lima. The district, settled by land takeovers, barely existed when I left but now teemed with a million or so mostly Andean migrants—all struggling to eke out a living at the edge of the city. Many homes in my neighborhood had no running water, some properties had walls of woven straw, and telephones were communal. It was an impoverished but hardworking area, full of striving, ambitious people. San Juan de Lurigancho, to most Limeños, is synonymous with the prison there. For this reason, it has an undeserved reputation as one of the more violent districts of Lima. The discrimination is such that when applying for work many young people give addresses in other parts of the city so they'll get a fair shot. It's a place where people demonstrate startling ingenuity when it comes to matters of survival and a place on the front lines of this stark cultural change.

Cynthia Bonifacio Rosales

My father

These are not just empty words or pseudo-social science. Here at the edge of a Third World capital, in a slum that had gone from sparsely populated to overpopulated in what amounts to an eye blink, everything was in flux. I'll give an example: One of my students was named Jhon Lennon Mariño Yupanqui. Everyone knew him as Lennon. He was sixteen and—like a lot of kids that age in the neighborhood (and in the world)—he was indifferent to school, nervous around girls, and not that concerned about his future. He worked with his old man a few days a week in a metal shop, did a few odd jobs for spending ▸

A Slum, a Boy Named Lennon, Some Dancing in the Street—Peru Revisited ***(continued)***

cash, and slept late as often as he could—even if this meant missing school. He was funny and charming and bright. And then there was that name. Lennon claimed, rather improbably, not to know of his namesake. I didn't buy it. The Beatles are founders of the global music canon—their songs are hummed at birthday parties in Egypt and China and Uruguay. When pressed, Lennon allowed that his parents "were fans"—and left it at that. He didn't seem to give it much thought, but of course I did. His name accomplished a kind of balancing act. It combined the indigenous heritage, the colonial legacy, and the thoroughly globalized Latin American present (misspelled, of course, or corrected for the Latin American ear—depending on your perspective).

"One of my students was named Jhon Lennon Mariño Yupanqui. Everyone knew him as Lennon."

César Ortiz Candia

Watch those hands

It became emblematic for me—a shorthand for the reality I was seeing. It's been said that the defining characteristic of Third World cities is that people live simultaneously in different centuries. Certainly this was true of my neighborhood. The man who lived at the corner was mayor of a town in Ayacucho that he visited just twice a year. His mother spoke only Quechua, an indigenous language, and hid out of sight whenever I visited. She would only speak to family members. There were dozens of women like her, wandering the neighborhood like ghosts, speaking only to those they knew. At the end of the block a family had converted their front room into a video game parlor where Lennon and his friends gathered in the evenings to play a pirated version of a Japanese dancing game. My street emptied into the market (which in the afternoon was also the soccer field), where chickens were deplumed and butchered beside a merchant who sold Manchester United jerseys—fakes of the very highest quality. Across the street, Ilvia's family had converted to Mormonism and all the girls were jealous because she was visited periodically by tall, handsome Americans. Omar liked to spend his free time on-line, chatting under the name Omar Smith because more girls responded that way. One young man spread the rumor that I was pishtaco (a mythical Andean demon), an outsider who comes to steal the organs of indigenous people. César from the next block had a younger sister who'd been adopted by American missionaries and was being raised in Minnesota. Sometimes he'd bring me letters she'd written and have me translate them. Kids played volleyball in the afternoons. After dark some gathered on the soccer field ▸

“My street emptied into the market (which in the afternoon was also the soccer field), where chickens were deplumed and butchered beside a merchant who sold Manchester United jerseys—fakes of the very highest quality.”

A Slum, a Boy Named Lennon, Some Dancing in the Street—Peru Revisited
(continued)

to get high. Koky stood guard over the street, his headphones always on and his eyes always red. He worked part-time in a factory that made white dress shirts for export—shirts just like the ones the Mormons wore.

And on and on. The neighborhood and its young people occupied this strange middle space. On Thursday afternoons we gathered at Lennon's house to listen to music, and everyone would practice their moves for Friday night. The music of choice was not rock or Andean or even salsa (that pan-Latin American rhythm)—it was trance that really moved them. Lennon set up mirrors so they could admire themselves, and everyone danced in the street. If a girl walked by, everything would momentarily stop, then start again with more fervor—they were watching! The kids taught each other new moves and learned them clumsily until they were perfected. Lennon rigged up a microphone and this was passed around, each one in turn mimicking the reggae-inflected rhymes that they heard at the club. I flirted briefly with

“Lennon set up mirrors so they could admire themselves, and everyone danced in the street.”

Brigit Recuay Denegri

My cousins

neighborhood stardom one afternoon by kicking an old Nas rhyme—"New York State of Mind"—that left Lennon and the rest breathless.

Has it always been this unsteady, this fragile? San Juan de Lurigancho is a place that has to be seen to be believed—and even then it's mystifying. The more I talked with young people like Lennon, the more my neighborhood seemed like a way station and everyone was just passing through. Their parents had come, scratched out a meager living, and passed the baton. Lennon and his generation were duty-bound to take it just a little bit further.

Lennon was still young, and so didn't have the urgency that some of the older kids had when he asked me about the United States. I was peppered with questions. Everyone talked hopefully of emigrating—of packing up and moving. Everyone had this notion of disappearing into the First World and returning with sacks of money. Lennon was no different than the rest—as misinformed, unrealistic and hopeful as any of them. It was something they learned very young. I once saw a group of children pushing toy trucks in the sandy street stop at the sound of a passing airplane and watch it fly overhead in reverent silence. It was only when it had passed that they thought to shout "Take me! Take me!" The older kids talked about scholarships, learning English, or marrying a Mormon— ►

A Slum, a Boy Named Lennon, Some Dancing in the Street—Peru Revisited
(continued)

but at heart the sentiment wasn't very different at all.

Most of the stories in *War by Candlelight* were written in the year after I returned from Lima. Now, as I reread them, I remember how urgent the process felt—trying to capture in words the energy of the city, the peculiar movement and tone of a place where everything is contingent on something else and the future is opaque and unknowable. Lima, of course, is only the Peruvian iteration of a global phenomenon. If I were Nigerian or Pakistani or Mexican, I could have written a very similar book—the place names changed, some altered details of the cultural landscape, but the essence would have been the same: an urban center defined by unbounded growth, social, political and economic instability, and dramatic cultural change. If Peru were an invented country, and Lima an imaginary city created for the purposes of this book, it would still be recognizable to many people around the world.

“Most of the stories in *War by Candlelight* were written in the year after I returned from Lima. Now, as I reread them, I remember how urgent the process felt.”

And if we can be certain of anything, it is that the lines will continue to blur. As an American of Latin American descent I find it increasingly difficult to tell where Latin America begins and where North America ends. José is one of the most common names for newborns in California (the state where I live). But back in Lima—in San Juan de Lurigancho—traditional Hispanic names are no longer in fashion: my friends had names like Roller, Norbert, and Hamilton. This state of flux provides the backdrop for the collection. All the characters inhabit these places of unstable identities, fluid geographies, and artificial boundaries. It's a state of mind I know well.

So it should come as no surprise that Andean musicians play the subways of New York, or that Mexicans work the pork plants of Iowa. It's no surprise that salsa outsells ketchup in the United States, or that a plurality of Peruvians want to emigrate. This is the world in which we live today. In Tucson, Arizona, a Thai family took over an old barbeque joint decorated with panoramic vistas of the Grand Canyon. They painted Buddhist temples and dramatic coiling dragons in the middle of the desert landscape. It took staring through an entire meal for me to figure out what they had done—and when I did I smiled from ear to ear and very nearly wanted to weep. The effect was as disconcerting as it was beautiful—something like a visual counterpart to my friend Lennon's absurdly meaningful name.

All photographs were taken by young Peruvians participating in a project Alarcón directed in Lima.

Author's Picks
Ten Powerful Books from the Latin American Canon

CONVERSATION IN THE CATHEDRAL
by Mario Vargas Llosa

In a conversation between two men over beers, Vargas Llosa analyzes the mental and moral mechanisms that govern power and the people behind it. More than a historic analysis of Peru, this is a groundbreaking novel that tackles questions of Latin American identity and how the lack of freedom can forever scar a people and a nation.

"*Conversation in the Cathedral* is a groundbreaking novel that tackles questions of Latin American identity and how the lack of freedom can forever scar a people and a nation."

THE FOX FROM ABOVE, THE FOX FROM BELOW
by José María Arguedas

Published after the author's suicide in 1969, *The Fox from Above, the Fox from Below* is set in the large fishing port of Chimbote, Peru. Arguedas depicts the struggle of the peasants of the Andean mountains who attempt to succeed in a country in the midst of a capitalist boom.

2666 by Roberto Bolaño

Bolaño's most ambitious novel—which he completed shortly before his untimely death due to illness—is separated into five distinct novellas. Each is connected by the mysterious murders of hundreds of Mexican women in a small town near the U.S.-Mexican border.

A UNIVERSAL HISTORY OF INIQUITY
by Jorge Luis Borges

Borges' earliest work is a collection of stories that takes the reader on a series of adventures around the world—including the corrupted street of Buenos Aires, the slave-owning South, and feudal Japan.

THREE TRAPPED TIGERS
by Guillermo Cabrera Infante

Set in pre-Castro Cuba, this grand and extremely smart novel has been called "a sexier, funnier, more readable Cuban *Ulysses.*"

"Set in pre-Castro Cuba, *Three Trapped Tigers* has been called 'a sexier, funnier, more readable Cuban *Ulysses.*'"

HOPSCOTCH by Julio Cortázar

In this novel the reader follows the many adventures of Horacio Oliveira, an expatriate writer who has just returned to his native Argentina from Paris and finds himself in eccentric situations as the keeper of a circus cat, a salesman, and an insane-asylum worker.

BURNT WATER by Carlos Fuentes

Fuentes vividly depicts the influence of class on Mexican society in this collection of novellas. His lively and often raw language takes the reader from the Mexican revolution to the Mexico of the sixties and seventies.

THE HEART THAT BLEEDS
by Alma Guillermoprieto

This collection of essays by Mexican journalist Guillermoprieto (originally published in *The New Yorker*) portrays the various struggles of Latin American countries as they evolve

Author's Picks ***(continued)***

into global capitalist nations. She addresses issues of class, race, and intergenerational conflict.

PEDRO PÁRAMO by Juan Rulfo

First published in 1955, this surrealist novel set in Mexico is the story of a man who must find his long lost father and—along the way—uncover his heritage. One of the first modern Latin writers to use magic realism, Rulfo was a major influence on Latin American literature.

"Juan Rulfo was one of the first modern Latin writers to use magic realism."

A FUNNY DIRTY LITTLE WAR
by Osvaldo Soriano

This political satire is set in a small village in postwar Argentina which goes into chaos after city leaders are charged with being "Marxist-Communists." In one day there are shootings, assassinations, and bombings—leaving the city in ruins.